"GET OUT! THIS IS PRIVATE PROPERTY."

Kat stiffened at the sound of the deep-voiced warning. She might have known this would happen, she mused humorlessly. But who ever said going home would be easy?

"I can hardly trespass in my own home, can I?" she asked as she forced herself to turn. She heard the man's sharply drawn breath.

"Kat?" Her name was a mere whisper.

"Hello, Jordan." She forced her voice to be calm, though she gazed at him hungrily. Suddenly there was a lump of guilt—and regret—in her throat.

"It's been a long time," he said evenly. His brown eyes pierced her, eyes that could light with humor or burn with passion, eyes that were now devoid of emotion. At that moment, Kat knew he had neither forgotten nor forgiven, and she felt a little part of her die once more . . .

CANDLELIGHT ECSTASY CLASSIC ROMANCES

CANDLELIGHT ECSTASY ROMANCES®

DECEPTION
AND DESIRE

Suzannah Davis

A CANDLELIGHT ECSTASY ROMANCE®

Published by
Dell Publishing Co., Inc.
1 Dag Hammarskjold Plaza
New York, New York 10017

ISBN: 0-440-11754-2

Printed in the United States of America

June 1987

10 9 8 7 6 5 4 3 2 1

WFH

*To Diane, Florence, and Mary Beth,
for believing.
Thank you, ladies!*

*Special thanks to Terry Pelletier Adcock of
Red River Farms in Coushatta, Louisiana,
and the owners, Joe and Jay Adcock.*

To Our Readers:

We have been delighted with your enthusiastic response to Candlelight Ecstasy Romances®, and we thank you for the interest you have shown in this exciting series.

In the upcoming months we will continue to present the distinctive sensuous love stories you have come to expect only from Ecstasy. We look forward to bringing you many more books from your favorite authors and also the very finest work from new authors of contemporary romantic fiction.

As always, we are striving to present the unique, absorbing love stories that you enjoy most—books that are more than ordinary romance. Your suggestions and comments are always welcome. Please write to us at the address below.

Sincerely,

The Editors
Candlelight Romances
1 Dag Hammarskjold Plaza
New York, New York 10017

DECEPTION
AND DESIRE

PROLOGUE

He sought the house eagerly, drawn by the light, the music, the sounds of laughter, and her. It was her birthday, and in his pocket he carried the tiny box holding the symbol of his love.

He walked across the uneven board porch, amazed once more at the love and life that surrounded the little house, even with its peeling paint and shabby imperfections. It was so different from his parents' house where boy and man were afraid to lounge in the stylish but uncomfortable furniture, and hothouse flowers were always exquisitely arranged; there were never yellow black-eyed Susans carelessly stuffed into a canning jar.

From the side of the porch the soft glow of a pipe caught his eye, and he hesitated, then nodded gravely to her grandfather standing quietly in the shadows. He never knew what to say these days, when family loyalties warred with the dictates of his heart.

"Go on in, boy," the old man said gruffly. "You're missing all the fun."

He plucked open the screen door and stepped inside. The noisy room vibrated with rock music and the sounds of celebration. He paused, his eyes drawn inexorably to her, barely noticing the other guests. She was like a golden flame as she danced, her warm honey-colored hair caught up in crimson ribbons that matched the embroidery on her cotton Mexican dress. Her long, slender legs were tied up in a crisscrossing of red leather sandal straps and she swayed and whirled to the music. He smiled involuntarily, bemused once more by her vibrancy, her gift of joy and life.

"Rusty!"

She reached for him and drew him into the midst of the crowd. Her blue eyes were bright, almost feverish, and her lips smiled so beautifully he thought he would die of wanting her. God, how he loved her!

"It came!" She laughed with delight, then dug into her pocket and waved a crumpled envelope under his nose.

"You goose! What came?" he asked expectantly as his heart swelled with pride and love.

"My acceptance. I'll go to Chapel Hill this fall! Isn't it wonderful?"

"What?" He felt the blood drain out of his head, his breath stop.

"I can't wait. But there's so much to do! I need clothes, and—"

"Wait." He caught her shoulders to get her attention. He shook his head to clear it. "I don't understand. What—what about us? What about our plans?" The little box burned his thigh through the denim of his jeans.

"Oh, Rusty!" She laughed, her mouth a flirtatious moue. "You didn't really think . . . all that talk . . . just talk . . . just a summer thing . . ."

He heard her from a distance as a great roaring seemed to fill his ears.

"Don't do this, kitten," he mumbled, swallowing hard on his fear. "It's not funny."

"Oh, dear," she murmured, her eyes wide and innocent. Her gaze dropped and she twisted the envelope, then shoved it deep into her pocket. "You didn't really think I was ready to get married, did you? Besides, I could never marry a man whose father is . . . well, dishonest."

12

Pain and rage and icy contempt battered inside him, hammering to be released. But he had always been taught the value of self-control, the importance of saving face, of keeping up appearances. He strangled on his impotent anger and choked on the biting agony of betrayal. Hatred roiled up within him, and he knew if he stayed another moment his hands would close on her throat and throttle the life he loved so dearly from her.

He turned with a snarl and pushed his way through the dancers who continued in their revelry as though nothing at all had happened.

She watched him leave, the animation draining from her features by degrees until her face was an expressionless mask. Only her eyes betrayed her, and they grieved silently. When the screen door slammed shut behind him, she walked quietly from the room, down the short hall to the bath, then shut and locked the door.

Paper rustled and her hand clenched around the tattered envelope in her pocket. She pulled it out, removed the enclosed paper and smoothed it out with great care. She stared at the blank sheet a long time, silent tears coursing down her cheeks.

She meticulously tore the paper and envelope into precise, geometric squares, then dropped them into the toilet. She watched the evidence of her innocence disappear and her whisper was raw with bitter despair.

"I hope you're satisfied, Rosalind. I hope you're satisfied."

CHAPTER ONE

The late-afternoon Louisiana sun streamed through the dirt-streaked windows of the little house, silhouetting the slim woman against the dust motes flung up by her passage into the familiar sitting room. With each step Katherine Holt moved back into time, passing the overloaded bookshelves, the sagging sofa, trailing her fingers over the scarred metal desk groaning under the weight of Papa John's old Royal typewriter. An overwhelming nostalgia carried her back, stripping away the evidence of years of neglect, transforming the room into the beloved haven of her memory.

Home. She was home at last.

The sound of a car's engine broke her reverie. Kat tipped her head, letting her wide straw hat brim shade her blue eyes from the dazzle. She wrinkled her nose. The room smelled stale, of mold and mice and long disuse, and already the heat made it like an oven although it was only May. Kat's wheat linen dress, chosen for coolness and comfort with its halter neckline and full skirt, clung to her sticky skin.

Heavy footsteps sounded on the warped boards of the wide porch, and the front door creaked.

"Get out. This is private property."

Kat stiffened at the sound of the deep-voiced warning.

Her grip automatically tightened on the straps of her precious cameras and their weight dug into her sore shoulder.

"I said you're trespassing," the voice repeated.

Reluctantly, Kat's lips twitched. She gave a small tired sigh, the long flight, the bandaged wound on her shoulder, and the man behind her taking their toll.

She might have known, she mused humorlessly. She might have known there would be no grace period before this happened. But whoever said going home would be easy?

Slowly, neck bent to one side, she tugged the hat from her head, freeing the honey-colored mass of her hair so it fell in silky abundance to her shoulders. She tossed her head and ran her fingers under the damp strands at her nape, postponing the inevitable moment when she'd have to turn and face this man for the first time in eleven long years.

"I can hardly trespass in my own home, can I?" she asked at last, forcing herself to turn. She heard his sharp, indrawn breath.

"Kat?" Her name was a mere whisper of sound.

"Hello, Jordan." Kat forced her voice to be calm though her stomach was suddenly shaken by tremors. Her eyes raked him hungrily, noting the changes the years had made, and there was suddenly a thick lump of guilt—and regret—in her throat.

Had he always been so tall? she wondered, letting her gaze rise up his long, rangy length. She smiled at the lock of hair that still fell rebelliously over his broad forehead. It was dark brown, the color of strong Louisiana coffee, and tipped with the faintest hint of auburn. He'd always been self-conscious about that bit of red, she remembered, as if it called too much attention to him, the stalwart and dutiful son of Senator and Mrs. Andrew Scott. How Kat had loved to tease him about it.

Oh, Rusty, is it really you?

16

"It's been a long time," he said. His eyes pierced her, eyes the color of caramel and toffee, eyes that could light sweetly with good humor or burn with passion, eyes now cold and devoid of emotion. At that moment Kat knew he had neither forgotten nor forgiven. It was an added complication to her life that she didn't need.

"Yes, a long time," she echoed, easing the cameras and duffel bag from her shoulder and setting them on the dusty floor. She couldn't hold back the involuntary grimace of pain and touched the tender skin with her fingertips. She saw Jordan's thick dark eyebrows lift in silent inquiry, his eyes trace the outline of the white bandage peeking from the edge of her bodice. Abruptly, Kat couldn't stand his scrutiny and turned away, tossing her hat onto the tangled pile of her meager luggage.

"Tell me, Jordan," she asked lightly, "are you always so protective of your neighbor's property? I was hardly out of the cab and in the door before you arrived."

Jordan made a restless movement and his muscles bunched under the white cotton of his dress shirt. A carefully understated tie was loosened at his neck, revealing his dark swarthy skin and the crisp curling hair on his chest.

"Whether you like it or not, Katherine, I've always kept an eye on the place. I was on my way home when I saw the open door. I thought some kids had broken in."

Puzzled, Kat didn't know what to make of his apparent concern. If he was truly as antagonistic as he appeared, why take the trouble? But she couldn't ask him that. Instead, she murmured, "Home?"

"I live on the farm now."

The farm. Kat's memories burned. She had grown up next door to the Scott Thoroughbred Breeding Farm, had worked there part time during her teenage years, had learned to love Jordan there during the Scott family's jaunts between Louisiana and Washington. She thrust the memory away. What she'd done, she'd had to do, she

17

thought angrily. But the price she'd paid had been high and she had carried her burden of guilt long enough. All she wanted now was peace. But she hadn't counted on Jordan's presence a mere half mile down the road.

Her mouth tightened and her voice was mocking. "Aren't you using that fancy law degree these days?"

"I have an office in Mansfield, but the farm takes a lot of my time."

"I guess the Bossier City track has helped the farm," she murmured, walking to a window. Jordan's eyes followed her as she slipped the latch and tried to tug it open.

"Yes, sometimes so much so it's hard to keep up with it. Living at the farm I can oversee everything."

"How—convenient." Kat panted, struggling with the stubborn sash. "And your mother? How is she?" Kat kept her eyes averted as she asked this seemingly innocuous question. She was reluctant to let Jordan see the residual hostility she still felt for her old enemy.

"She's living in town and doing well, though she misses Dad." Jordan's father had died eight or nine years before, Kat knew. A senator of his status had been widely eulogized in the press.

Jordan made a small annoyed sound in his throat, and stepped closer, adding his strength to her efforts. The window sash popped, then slid up with a protesting shriek. A gentle breeze eddied into the stuffy room, bringing with it the resiny odor of the grove of pines behind the house and the faint, sweet smell of honeysuckle.

Kat tensed and her heart drummed at Jordan's nearness. She caught a whiff of a citrusy cologne and male end-of-the-day musk. This close, she could see the shadow of his dark beard and had to fight the sudden urge to run her palm down his lean cheek to test the rasp against her own skin. She closed her eyes and swallowed. She must be losing her mind to even think such a thing! There was too much bad blood between them.

18

Jordan looked down at Kat, his face impassive, but his mind was still reeling with the shock of seeing her so unexpectedly after all these years. Damn it! Why had she returned? She was more beautiful than ever, slim and graceful in a flowing dress, the skirt unbuttoned to mid-thigh as if to flaunt her long, lovely legs. There were tiny laugh lines at the corners of her eyes, but otherwise her face was as unmarked and dewy as it had been when she was a teenager. And her eyes, large and sparkling blue with a band of violet around the iris, so open and compelling a man could lose his soul in them still. The slight bump on the bridge of her upturned nose kept her from the purity of a classic profile, yet it somehow gave her more life, more vivacity than other women.

His eyes moved to the tooled Moroccan leather belt that cinched her slender waist, and the matching brass-studded bangle she wore on her wrist next to a chunky stainless steel watch. She still had a flair for the unusual, a sense of style that transcended fashion to make her own individual statement, but now it was softened, more sophisticated. Even in her simple dress she carried an air of big-city glamour. She had always been a free spirit. It had been one of the things that had attracted him most—until that day she rejected him. He felt a sickening churning of emotions so long buried he'd thought they had died.

He noticed the pallor of her skin, the purplish shadows beneath her eyes, and his glance again went to the telltale gauze on her shoulder. What the hell had happened to her? Something low in his gut twisted at the thought of her hurt, her creamy, well-remembered flesh torn and bloody. Her pulse beat rapidly at the base of her throat, and unbidden, memories of his lips pressed there and the taste and texture of her skin overwhelmed him.

Oh, no, Kat, not again, he vowed silently. Ruthlessly, he consigned the vision to the past and allowed his anger to take control.

19

"All right, Katherine," he demanded, "what are you really doing here?"

"I've come home," she said. Her fingers worried nervously at the oversized gold loop earring, a gesture Jordan recognized. The fact that he did irritated him unreasonably.

He frowned. "For how long?"

"To stay. Not that it's any of your business," she added defiantly.

The setting sun dimmed the room and cast shadows across the austere planes of Jordan's face. He allowed a harsh, disbelieving laugh to escape him. "Don't tell me you're giving up the life of a globe-trotting news photographer? As I recall you couldn't leave this 'podunk' town fast enough."

"I have my reasons," Kat replied. She stepped away from his cutting words, crossed to the kitchen doorway and futilely flicked a light switch. "Damn," she muttered.

She went into the kitchen and began to search through the cabinets, aware that Jordan followed her. She located kitchen matches and a candle stub, and turned, only to find Jordan blocking her path.

"What would make you desperate enough to come back to Mansfield?" he wondered aloud. He touched the edge of the bandage with a light fingertip. "What happened?"

Kat felt a frisson of heat race along her spine at his touch and impatiently shrugged his hand away. "My last assignment was in Lebanon. I caught a fragment of a car bomb. My partner was killed."

"You were lucky, then." Jordan felt a chill race through him at the image her monotone words evoked.

"Yes. Lucky." Her voice was emotionless. There was no way to explain to him the devastation and utter bleakness she had felt after that violence. Ultimately she had decided to resign her job with a Washington-based news bureau and come home to Mansfield to seek a new life. No, there was

20

no way to explain it, not when she could feel his bitterness and condemnation hovering between them, so she didn't even try.

She stepped past him, lit the candle with shaking fingers and set it in a cracked saucer on the dinette table. She stared across the flickering flame into his face and taunted him in a gentle voice. "Well, Jordan? Aren't you going to say 'welcome home'?"

"You expect me to be overjoyed that you've come home to lick your wounds? Think again, Katherine." His reply was careless, casual—and hurtful.

"I don't expect anything from you," Kat snapped. "So if you'll excuse me . . ." Her eyebrows lifted expectantly.

"You can't mean to stay here tonight?"

"Why not?" she challenged.

"No power, no water." He looked at the abandoned, dirty clutter of a house that no one had lived in for ten years. He jammed his fists into his pants pockets and his face was grim, but resolute. "Let me take you somewhere."

"Why, counselor! Is that a proposition?" Kat laughed, real amusement in her tone.

Jordan's mouth compressed in an annoyed line. "Bertie still keeps house for me. She'd be glad to have you."

"Aunt Bertie?" Kat's mouth curved into a smile of loving remembrance, showing her fondness for the woman who had been like a mother to her in many ways. "I'd love to see her again," she admitted.

"She always wondered why she never heard from you after you went to college."

Again a lump of guilt thickened Kat's throat. "After Papa John died, I . . . I thought it was best."

"A clean break, right, Katherine?" Jordan's tone held a wealth of bitterness. "Nothing messy from your past to slow you down on your rise to the top."

"It wasn't like that—" She broke off and gave herself a mental shake. "I don't have to explain myself to you."

21

His fist slammed down hard on the tabletop, making the candle flame weave manically. "You're damned right! But you never were very good at explanations, were you?"

Kat jumped at his violent movement, then licked her lips nervously. Her heart thudded frantically against her chest. She almost laughed. Here she was, the fearless Kat Holt, the woman who would take any assignment, no matter how tough, deal with fanatics or statesmen, no matter how powerful, yet she was suddenly afraid. Afraid of this man she'd wronged through no fault of her own other than being too young to find other options. Afraid of the physical attraction that seemed to have grown more powerful instead of weakening, and afraid of the harsh light in Jordan's eyes that spoke of revenge, a revenge that could easily be his because no matter what she told herself, she hadn't stopped caring.

Still, it was almost a relief to have his hostility out in the open. She sank down on a chair. "What do you want from me, Jordan?" she asked wearily. "That was all a long time ago. Your father's malfeasance trial, and Papa John and the newspaper campaign. Scott versus Holt. Holt versus Scott. What chance did we have?"

Jordan braced his fists on the table and leaned across it to glare down at her upturned face. "None, but that was your choice. So tell me, Kat, was it worth it?"

She glanced away, feeling the sting of tears behind her eyes. He had every right to hate her. Yes, she'd turned her back on him, but he would never know it had been a sacrifice of love.

"Well, was it worth it?" Jordan demanded again. "Tell me you have no regrets."

"It was something I had to do," was all she could say. She swallowed, looked back at him, then tentatively laid her hand across his clenched fist. "I never meant to hurt you. I know I never said it then, but for what it's worth, Jordan—I'm sorry."

"It's not worth a damn, lady, and you know it!" His voice was harsh and he jerked his hand free as though her touch burned him.

Kat despaired then, knowing she would never be able to explain, not without inflicting more pain. She would not devastate him with the truth that the family he loved and whose welfare he had always put above his own had betrayed his loyalty. She sighed, feeling totally drained, knowning that forgiveness was not in him. "I don't want us to be enemies, Jordan. After all, we are neighbors."

"But not friends. Not any longer."

"All right!" Kat snapped, angry at his stubbornness. Was mere civility too much to expect? She glared at him, her eyes flashing like blue flames. "I'm not asking anything from you. Just stay out of my way and I'll stay out of yours."

"Do you really think that's possible in a town this size?"

"I'll make a point of it!"

Jordan leaned closer, and Kat felt the warm whisper of his breath on her forehead. "You're just fooling yourself." His brown eyes looked almost black. "Don't stay. You don't belong here anymore."

His words chilled her, but she lifted her chin, defiantly meeting his gaze. Her voice was soft and fierce with determination. "This is my home. I won't let you drive me away."

"There's nothing here for you," Jordan replied. "You were always a little too wild, a little too far out for this town. Face it, Katherine, you're too glamorous, too worldly. You've outgrown us. What makes you think you'll be accepted now? What makes you think you're even wanted?"

Kat paled. She stood, scraping back the chair, her jaw and fists clenched. "That's despicable. Not everyone fits into tidy little black and white boxes. Others might bow to the Scott power and money, but not me—not again! Now get out of my house!"

Jordan frowned, fighting the explosive anger that threatened to erupt, fighting the lurking admiration at her defiance, fighting the impulse to take her in his arms and kiss her until they were both breathless. Willful self-control won the battle. Abruptly, he turned on his heel and stalked back through the house.

Kat quivered as the tension left her body and she sat back down, burying her face in her hands. It was time to admit the truth. Her longing to be home again, among familiar places, familiar people, was only part of the reason she had come back to Mansfield. Deep down, in her soul of souls, she'd hoped to find something she had once lost, a flicker of something in Jordan that would indicate his softer feelings for her hadn't been completely extinguished.

Fool! she berated herself. *What were you hoping for, a fairy-tale ending?*

She listened to Jordan's angry retreat from the house. Then he paused on the porch and retraced his steps to the kitchen. She kept her face in her palms, her hair falling around her face like a shield.

"Get up. You're coming with me," he said from the doorway.

"Go to hell."

"I'm not going to leave you here alone tonight. This place isn't habitable."

She dropped her hands and slowly scanned the darkening kitchen with its uneasy shadows. "I've been in worse."

His laugh was low, humorless. "I'll bet. But it makes no difference. Come on." He crossed and caught her upper arm to urge her to her feet.

"Get your hands off me!" She wrenched free, then gasped, doubling over at the stab of pain in her shoulder.

"Kat!" Jordan dropped to one knee, an arm braced behind her for support. "Are you all right?"

Kat exhaled and the throbbing began to subside. "I'm okay." She uncurled carefully, resting against his arm. Her expression was wry. "The stitches just came out."

"I'm sorry," he said, contrite. Their faces were on the same level and their eyes locked and held for an interminable moment. It seemed so much needed to be said, yet neither had the words to say it.

"Oh, Jordan," Kat whispered at last, her lips trembling. Hesitantly, her hand rose to touch his lean jaw with a light caress. She was anguished, yet helpless. "Weren't there any good times?"

His eyes darkened and he looked away. "I only remember the worst."

Hopelessly, Kat's hand fell away. She straightened and Jordan stood.

"Are you coming?"

The fight went completely out of Kat. After eleven years she finally accepted that there was no going back for her and Jordan. "All right," she answered at last, surprising him. "Will you take me back to the motel in town?"

"If you like."

"Thank you." Suddenly they were as formal and polite as newly introduced strangers.

Kat looked around once more while Jordan efficiently gathered up her equipment. The little house had been a home once, and could be again with a little love and elbow grease. It was all she had left. And it was all she needed, she told herself firmly.

She cupped her hand around the flame and blew out the candle, then followed Jordan out to his car, a sleek silver Mercedes SL. She was silent and withdrawn as they drove the five miles into Mansfield, her thoughts busy. At least she knew exactly where she stood with Jordan now and could lay those nebulous hopes and dreams to rest. She could play the role of polite acquaintance. In fact, it suited

25

her just fine, she assured herself. There was no use stirring up feelings dead and buried long ago.

She tried to ignore the firm clasp of his tanned hands on the steering wheel, tried to concentrate on other things. Like how to earn a living with her cameras, and how to find the inner peace that had so long eluded her in the hurly-burly world of news bureau photography. She tried to convince herself that here, at home in the slower-paced South, she could go back to her roots to find the things she needed to rebuild her life. She tried not to notice how the rolled cuffs of his shirt made a stark contrast to the dark skin of his sinewy forearms.

The years had lain a veneer of sophistication over this intimate stranger, an aura of leashed power and virility veiled by a vague familiarity. Unwanted, unexpectedly, she felt the strength of that aura in the confining space of the car. She glanced toward him, found his eyes on her, and hastily looked away, nearly breathless. Despite everything, there was still that invisible tug of attraction that had always been between them. Jordan Scott was still the most attractive man she had ever known.

Jordan urged a bit more speed from the powerful engine, then forced his foot off the accelerator. There was no point in getting a ticket just because being this close to Kat Holt was making him more uncomfortable by the second. He couldn't seem to keep his eyes off the tantalizing slice of calf and thigh revealed by her skirt. She was even more beautiful than he remembered, although remembering was a luxury he rarely allowed himself. But she wasn't the girl of his memories, either; she was all woman, mature, subtle, self-assured. Just looking at her tugged at his heartstrings and made him dizzy. He knew he was slowly going crazy. He had to get away from her soon, before he did something foolish.

The proprietors along Polk Street had turned off the lights and closed up for the night. He turned down Washington and headed for the motel. At least Kat would have a decent room tonight.

His jaw hardened and he cursed himself inwardly. Dammit! He would *not* care what happened to her! He wouldn't let himself. Never again!

He pulled into the small parking lot. "I'll get you a room," he said gruffly. Garish-colored light from the motel's sign illuminated her downcast face. She looked up, and the moving arrow of light was reflected in her wide blue eyes.

"That's all right. I can do it." She began to scramble for her cameras.

Jordan bit back an irritated expletive. "Still as stubborn as ever, I see. You're almost out on your feet. Stay where you are. I'll be right back."

"Still as bossy as ever, I see," she called as he walked away. Then with a sigh she fell back into the comfortable seat. He was right. She was so tired she could sleep for a week. Maybe if she did, when she woke up she wouldn't feel so depressed, wouldn't doubt the wisdom of her move back to Mansfield . . .

"Here you go."

Kat looked up to find Jordan dangling a key from his index finger. For an instant her mischievous sense of humor took over, and she wondered what the town gossips would say about Jordan taking a room at the motel for a "strange" woman. But he looked so grim she didn't share her thoughts. He had probably become a staid old sourpuss, she mused consolingly as she followed him to the door.

Jordan inserted the key and swung open the door to reveal a sterile room with two double beds and a chest of drawers. An air-conditioner hummed softly. Kat looked at the room with resigned dismay. She had run halfway across the world to end up alone again in yet another unwelcoming motel room. It didn't seem fair.

Dejectedly she stepped inside and placed her cameras on the bureau. Jordan set her duffel bag beside them and offered her the key.

"Thank you," she said, feeling stiff and awkward.

"Is there anything—"

"No, I'm sure I can manage."

He wouldn't ask her what she planned to do, Jordan promised himself.

Surely he would ask about her plans, Kat thought hopefully.

"Well," he began.

"Yes, ah, thank you."

"Good-bye, then." He hesitated, then his jaw firmed and he strode out the door.

" 'Bye, Jordan," she murmured after him. She closed the door, then stepped to the window beside it. Her hands paused on the drapery cords as she watched him climb into his car. Kat felt the old ache of misery steal out to attack her and send her mind hurtling back to that horrible time.

Rosalind Scott's reasonable, melodious voice seemed to mock her from the past, explaining over and over again how Kat "wasn't right" for Jordan, her sulfuric words making chinks in Kat's determination. Yet it hadn't been the family's plans for Jordan to attend a prestigious law school, nor even Rosalind's assurance that their relationship couldn't survive in the face of conflicting family loyalties that had made Kat turn Jordan away. Though Papa John and his newspaper had been the first to break the story about accusations of corruption against Senator Andrew Scott, it was almost over when Rosalind came to Kat that day.

"You realize that the senator will be acquitted, of course," Rosalind had said, chic and composed in her designer suit and sculpted hairdo.

"I'm glad, for Jordan's sake," Kat replied. "I'll be glad when it's over, Mrs. Scott."

"But it's far from over, Katherine," Jordan's mother said, her mouth squeezing into a sour, satisfied grimace. "I'm well aware of what's going on between you and Jordan, and I want it ended immediately!"

"Jordan loves me," Kat returned defiantly, a blush of warm color staining her cheeks. "And I love him!"

"That's ridiculous," Rosalind snapped. "I will not let Jordan sacrifice his future on a little nobody!"

"We're going to be married," Kat said stubbornly. "I'll be eighteen soon, and we're going to be together."

"Even at the expense of your grandfather?"

Kat sat in shocked disbelief as Rosalind proceeded to unveil her threats, explaining about the million-dollar libel suit that would be filed against Papa John the minute the senator was acquitted. How the high-powered lawyers would see to it that her grandfather, who had raised her alone, lost everything—the house, the newspaper, everything. And what would that do to John Holt's precarious health? Everyone knew he had that heart condition.

"You can't do that! He was only doing his job!" Kat sobbed desperately. "It could kill him!"

"I could persuade Andrew not to file the suit," Rosalind said with all the sweetness of a black widow spider. "But you know what I want in return, don't you, Katherine?"

Yes, she had known, and in the end there had been nothing else she could do but tell the lies and destroy Jordan's love. It had been months, years before she began to feel again after the devastation of losing him. Sometimes she wondered if she would ever be able to love again with that first purity and fire, and though she had had many friends, no man had ever been able to capture her heart again.

Jordan's car disappeared out of sight and Kat slowly drew the drapes, shutting out the neon glare of the flashing motel sign. No, there had been no special someone in her

29

life since she had sent Jordan out of it. And now she feared that she knew why. Fool that she was, she had never been able to forget that loving Jordan Scott was the best thing that had ever happened to her.

CHAPTER TWO

Kat mopped her sweaty forehead with a blue bandanna, then tied it bandit-style around her neck. She pushed untidy tendrils of honey-blond hair back into the knot on top of her head and surveyed the house with satisfaction. Four hours ago, armed with mop, broom, and cleaning supplies, she'd come to do battle with the grimy residue of ten years. Now she was the one who was grimy, but the floors were clean, the clutter had vanished, and the counters gleamed.

All the windows and doors stood open, admitting the sweet May morning, the sibilant chirpings of crickets and the raucous call of blue jays. Kat smiled. All in all it had been a very productive morning, from the battered '61 coupe she'd rented from Edgar Mosset to the timely arrival of Reggie Patterson in his utility company truck to turn on the power, to Mrs. Juanita Harvey's promise to provide a phone in "probably a week, not more than ten days." Why, she had even managed to prime the well pump single-handedly, and it hadn't taken more than half an hour to run the muck out of the tank and bring up the cold sparkling water. There was still a lot to be done, and she didn't even dare contemplate the disaster that had once been the yard, but she would sleep in the house that night. Home, at last.

In the kitchen, the refrigerator motor clanked and gurgled. Kat grimaced wryly and went to check on the reluctant appliance. The cans of grapefruit juice she'd placed there earlier were barely cool. Kat popped the top of one and sipped the tart liquid. It probably needed freon, she mused, mentally subtracting yet another expense from her rapidly shrinking bank account. The sooner she got her darkroom set up and properly equipped, the sooner she could begin to earn a living.

Kat had planned her strategy as she cleaned the house. She would free-lance, do a little portrait work, weddings, dance recitals, and the like. And if Mansfield lacked enough business to sustain her, there were always the twin river cities of Shreveport-Bossier just thirty miles away. Perhaps not as exciting as an overseas assignment, but just what she wanted, Kat thought, rubbing her shoulder absently. She would have to use a commercial photo lab until she could convert her old bedroom into a darkroom, and absently wondered how many gallons of black paint she'd need. Then there were the trays and chemicals, an enlarger, the list seemed endless—and expensive. It was a good thing her needs weren't great, but even so she would have to put every penny she had toward accomplishing her goal. It was clear that things would be tight financially, at least for a while, but that didn't worry her. Something would always turn up.

She tidily dropped the empty juice can into the garbage pail and stretched. Her shoulder ached, but not unpleasantly so. She rotated it, testing it gingerly, and was pleased by the returning ease of movement. Maybe exercise was what it needed, but she knew she'd done enough for the day. It was time for a break.

She walked out on the porch, her sneakers silent on the weathered boards. She rubbed her hands on the soft, faded denim of her jeans, then caught the hem of her large white T-shirt and knotted it at her hip. Jamming her hands palm out in her back pockets, she rocked restlessly on her heels.

She scanned the yard, gone wild with time, and her gaze

edged toward a familiar path leading through the pine thicket. She'd always used that path, now hardly more than a rabbit track, when she worked at Scott Farms, used it also to meet Jordan in their special place.

Kat frowned, pushing the image away. She wouldn't think about Jordan. To do so made her heart tighten painfully. From now on, all he was to her was a former acquaintance. She studied the path. It wouldn't hurt to explore it once again. If it were still passable she could look over the farm for old times' sake and drop in to see Aunt Bertie.

Kat's expression brightened. Bertie, whose homey soul had always held a welcome for her. There was a lot to make up for with Aunt Bertie, years of silence to repay. Had she changed much? Kat vaulted down the steps with sudden urgency. It was time to pay Aunt Bertie a call.

Ten feet along the path the underbrush thinned. Twenty feet and she walked through well-remembered woods, dappled with sunlight and a cool stillness. The hollow call of a tree owl echoed under the roof of the forest and Kat sniffed the pleasant odors of earth and living things. A sense of satisfaction grew within her. This was all hers now. It was twenty-three acres, a portion of it rough pasture land, but mostly pristine forest with a little creek meandering through its center. It was a legacy from Papa John, and one that was strangely soothing, peaceful. As she looked around Kat knew that she had done the right thing coming home, even if Jordan Scott had accused her of not belonging anymore.

It only took a few minutes to reach the boundary between her property and Scott Farms. The line was marked by a whitewashed board fence that seemed to stretch for endless miles around the neat paddocks filled with sleek thoroughbred mares and their long-legged foals. The old barn was freshly painted and several new auxiliary buildings had been built since the last time Kat had seen the farm. She slipped between the wooden rails of the fence

33

and made her way past the barn, noting with approval other improvements and obvious signs of prosperity. It was clear that under Jordan's management the thoroughbred brood farm was very successful.

Kat pondered this while following the lane leading toward the low-slung ranch-style house. Here again were signs of progress. The manicured lawn, the jut of a new wing, even the blue sparkle of a new swimming pool at the back. Suddenly she questioned the wisdom of coming here again. Her footsteps faltered. She was treading on thin ice, coming uninvited into Jordan's territory, knowing how he despised her. But he couldn't have any objections to her seeing Bertie, could he? Kat glanced at her watch. Surely Jordan was at his office this time of day. And she did want to see Bertie.

Kat quickened her steps, rounding the corner of the house and hurrying toward the back door. Beyond her was the spreading expanse of the new brick terrace surrounding the tiled swimming pool, the scene set off by cascades of red geraniums growing in large wooden barrels. It was a pretty sight, but Kat's attention was focused on the short, round figure of the gray-haired woman standing on the threshold, holding open the screen door in silent welcome.

"'Bout time you showed up," Bertha Simpson commented. "And mind you wipe your feet."

"Yes, ma'am." Kat grinned, fighting tears, and feeling sixteen again.

"Got some blueberry muffins ready to come out of the oven," Bertie announced, letting the door fall shut behind Kat. She bustled forward into the spacious country kitchen that had always been her domain. Kat couldn't feel uncomfortable about barging into Jordan's home because this room was so clearly Bertie's. "Well, don't just stand there," Bertie ordered, her voice strangely gruff. "You look like you could use some feeding up."

Kat followed, watching Bertie flit efficiently from oven to

table to sink and back. "I couldn't eat a bite," Kat said around a thick lump in her throat. "Not until I get a hug."

The older woman ceased her birdlike movements, her hazel eyes behind the gold wire rims of her eyeglasses startled, then sparkling with moisture. With the total efficiency that comprised all her movements, she enveloped Kat in a warm embrace, pulling the younger woman to her ample bosom in unquestioning affection.

"Oh, Aunt Bertie, it's so good to see you!" Kat choked.

"Jordan told me you was back."

"He did?" Kat questioned weakly. She looked down into the older woman's face, noticing the deepening lines, the abundance of gray in her short, curling hair. Time had taken its toll on Bertie and Kat felt a sudden stab of remorse. "Oh, Aunt Bertie, I'm sorry I didn't write, didn't call—"

"Hush, honey. It was all right. I understood. There's some places, some people best forgotten."

"But not you," Kat said ruefully. "I'm sorry."

Bertie smiled and patted Kat's back, soothing her as she'd done when Kat was just a little girl. Bertie rubbed a finger under the frame of her glasses, straightened her inconsiderable height, and spoke again with her usual pertness. "Will you look at us? Mewling like two ninnies! Come over here while I brew some tea. You and me, we got some catching up to do!"

Plied with tea and hot muffins dripping with butter, Kat gave Bertie a brief summary of the past ten years, ending with her decision to return to Mansfield, but carefully omitting any reference to Jordan.

"Can't say I'm not glad to have you back where you belong," Bertie said tartly, passing Kat another muffin. Kat smiled with pleasure. Here, at least, was someone who wanted her home. Bertie rattled on. "All that gallivanting! My lands! Who'd have ever thought?"

"I'm glad to be home, but I've got a lot to do," Kat

35

replied. "There's the advertising and photographic supplies to see about, and although I've made a dent inside the house, my yard is so grown up it looks like a jungle! But I know it'll be worth it." She felt replete, satisfied, and basked in the warm radiance of Bertie's nurturing and unquestioning acceptance.

"Well, it's the first lick of sense you've shown since—" Bertie broke off and began bustling about with the dishes, muttering to herself. "Never could understand you two young 'uns falling out that way. Never saw two folk more in love."

Kat stirred uncomfortably. "Bertie, please. That was a long time ago."

"All right, all right," Bertie said, tossing up her hands. "You know I never say anything. Though why you and Jordan couldn't patch things up now that you're back . . ."

"Jordan made it quite clear that he doesn't even like me anymore, so don't get any wild ideas," Kat warned.

Bertie made a noise that sounded suspiciously like a snort. "I know he ain't never got over you."

Kat felt a sudden pang at Bertie's words, an instant surge of hope that was quickly suppressed by the memory of Jordan's dislike and cold attitude the day before.

"Oh, I don't mean he's been a monk," Bertie continued. "He's a man, for sure. There's been a stream of his lady friends in and out of here, but not one of them has ever lasted any time at all. Course, a woman would have to be made of steel to withstand Mrs. Scott's third degree, anyway. Them little cream puffs he squires around don't stand a chance against her." She shot Kat a sharp glance. "Not like some I could mention."

Bertie would be amazed if she confessed she had melted like a cream puff once herself, Kat thought. But what else could she have done? She had been young and naïve, unable to fight back to keep what she wanted.

"I'm sure when Jordan finds someone he really wants, what Rosalind likes or doesn't like won't make any difference," Kat said stiffly, wondering why she defended him.

"Maybe. But you remember all her high-falutin' notions, and she hasn't lost one of them, especially where her son is concerned. She wants him to be a big shot, like his daddy was."

"Oh? And what does Jordan have to say about that?" Kat asked, casually drawing designs on the tabletop with a fingertip.

Bertie shrugged. "He don't have time to worry about Rosalind, mostly. What with trying to run a law practice, and it being the middle of breeding season and all. There've been mares foaling at all hours of the night, and one of them ding-blam hands up and left 'cause they was working him too hard." Bertie's voice oozed with contempt.

Kat laughed softly. "Things haven't changed very much."

" 'Cept there's just a lot more of everything," Bertie muttered. "Don't know why a body wants to take on more than he can handle."

"Because he loves it, I suppose. And from the looks of things, it must be going very well."

"Sure it is," Bertie said, her voice quivering with sarcasm. "But what good will it do the man if he don't live to enjoy it?"

Kat laughed again and hugged Bertie. "The question is, what would Jordan do if you weren't here to worry about him?"

"Go to rack and ruin, no doubt."

"No doubt," Kat agreed solemnly, but a twinkle of laughter glinted in her eyes. She dusted the muffin crumbs from her lap and gave a little sigh. "I'd better be going."

Laden with a napkin full of muffins and a promise to visit again soon, Kat retraced her steps down the lane. She cast an admiring eye over the scores of mares and their frisky offspring, but her steps faltered at the last paddock. She propped a foot on the bottom rung of the fence, placed the muffins on the top of the nearest post, and strained her eyes toward a single mare standing in the shade of a tree. Was that . . . could it be?

Jordan braked sharply, the rear of his car sliding on the gravel drive. Damn! When he was in a hurry, there always seemed to be something. He'd been late getting out of court and he knew his stud man, J.W., was waiting on him to help breed that mare just in from Kentucky, and now some skinny kid was draped across his fence. There were always folks passing by to admire the horses, but he took exception to anyone getting too close and upsetting the high-strung mares, especially this one.

He rolled down his window to suggest the kid keep his distance, but the words caught in his throat. His eyes narrowed, following the long line of jeans-clad leg up to where the faded fabric stretched tightly across a jutting hip—a female hip, a sweet, subtle set of curves just made to fill a man's hands. His throat tightened, and in answer so did another portion of his body. The unwanted response made him angry.

Kat turned on her perch, and her fierce frown matched Jordan's. The sunlight glinted off the golden knot on the back of her head, and soft tendrils lovingly caressed her flushed cheeks. Kat lightly jumped down from the fence as Jordan emerged from the car and she rounded on him like a small, indignant tornado.

"What have you done to her?" she demanded. "That's Sabrina, isn't it? What's the matter with her?"

For a moment Jordan's mind was blank with surprise. His gaze clashed with her stormy blue one, then dropped to where the faint rosy outline of her nipples thrust impudently forward under the thin cotton T-shirt. He groaned inwardly and tore his eyes away. Even disguised as a boy, with a smudge on her cheek, she still had the power to stir him, to arouse him against his will. His body wouldn't pay attention to the dictates of his mind, to the common sense that said this woman couldn't be trusted. It made him resentful and stoked his anger. Why the hell had she come back? Just to torment him, it seemed. He clenched his jaw.

"It's Sabrina," he acknowledged curtly. Lady Sabrina's Dream. The chestnut filly he and Kat had ushered into the world together one soft spring night. The horse had always been Kat's favorite, the one she'd petted and babied and spoiled just like a child. He shouldn't be surprised that she recognized the mare now. There had always been a special bond between the two of them. Which made Kat's concern understandable, even if long ago she'd given up that right, along with so many others.

"I don't understand. What's wrong? Why is she kept apart from the others?" Kat questioned. "Jordan, it's not fair—"

"She's blind, Katherine."

"No!" Kat's lips fell open on that whispered denial. She spun around, clambered up on the fence, straining forward to find the evidence of that harsh verdict. Her voice quavered. "Damn!"

Jordan moved to the fence beside her, sensing the pain quivering through her. "We sent her to Kentucky a few years ago to be bred, and somehow one eye was damaged," he explained gruffly. "Last breeding season, moon blindness finally took the other."

"Oh."

Her shoulders slumped in dejection and it took everything Jordan had not to reach out to her. But down that road lay danger and pain and all the things he'd sworn never to let her inflict on him again. His hands stayed clenched inside his pockets.

"She's adjusting. Normally she's with the other mares,

but I had her brought up here because she's due to foal shortly."

"You're still breeding her?" Kat turned a watery blue gaze to Jordan.

"Sure. She's one of my best mares. Only her sight is damaged. She breeds easily, usually has no trouble foaling, and her offspring bring top dollar. In fact, I've got a two-year-old of Sabrina's in training now. Dream Tender, we call her, and the trainer says she can fly."

"I suppose that's the best thing," Kat replied slowly. "But still . . ." She dabbed at the moist corners of her eyes with her fingertips and shrugged miserably. Jordan's eyes again dropped to the rounded outline of her breasts and his mouth went dry. His gaze moved upward, caught and held the liquid blue pools of her eyes, and something intangible sizzled in the air between them. Jordan's eyes dropped away self-consciously and a rosy tide stained Kat's cheeks. He cleared his throat and turned toward the paddock.

"See for yourself." Jordan pressed his tongue against his teeth and gave an ear-piercing whistle. Across the paddock the mare's ears twitched, and she started forward, following a well-worn path along the edge of the fence.

"I always wished I could whistle like that," Kat said in a tremulous voice. She half lay across the top of the fence, her heels rocking on the center rung, and looked back over her shoulder at Jordan with a wry, tentative smile. To her delight, he almost smiled back.

A reluctant rapport sprang up full-blown. Jordan felt her charm, the bewitching nostalgia of shared memories wooing him to forget what was past, to take the here and now. Her rounded bottom was on a level with Jordan's shoulder and it would have been a natural thing to steady her with a hand on her frayed back pocket, a thing he had done countless times. His palm tingled and his memories burned. Abruptly, he whistled again, forcing the surging feelings down with a ruthlessness that was his only hope of self-preservation.

Calling and whistling, Jordan's voice led the horse straight to them, and she hung her head over the fence, stamping and blowing to catch their scent.

"Hello, Sabrina," Kat said softly and offered her hand to be sniffed. She petted the mare's velvet nose. "Do you remember me?"

She crooned to the horse and Jordan watched her hands move, remembering, but trying not to. Remembering the feel of her cool fingers on his heated flesh, the tantalizing, feather-soft caresses that became bolder as her passion grew. They'd had their stolen, golden moments their first times. The first fumbling attempts, so saturated with heady emotion that technique was unimportant, feeling was all. The smooth pale expanse of her skin against his, the smell of ferns crushed beneath them and the soaring, spirit-dissolving explosion that bound them as one.

It all rushed back to Jordan as she stroked the mare's neck, and with it came the pain. Their relationship had meant everything to him, nothing to her. Confusion was like a black whirlpool that sucked him down, down until nothing was left but his anger. Why couldn't he be indifferent? After all these years, where was the studied neutrality, the unconcern he had cultivated so assiduously? He was shaken by his lack of control. All his defenses were threatened. The calm, logical order of his life was on the point of upheaval and he couldn't stand for that. The sooner Kat realized her mistake in returning to Mansfield and made another exit from his life, the better. If necessary, he'd give her the extra incentive needed to speed her on her way, far away from him before her insidious charms lured him into disaster again.

The mare nickered and Kat's soft laughter wafted skyward. Jordan steeled himself against the innocent, unguarded look of pleasure on her lovely, animated face.

"No, Saby, I haven't got a carrot. How about a blueberry muffin instead?" The muffin was crumbled and offered, then nosed and nibbled. Kat giggled as the mare's mobile lips tickled her open palm. "Look, Jordan! I think she remembers me!"

"Or your bribes. I see you've been up to the house."

At the sudden grimness of his tone, Kat shot him a cautious glance. She dusted the crumbs off her hands and dropped down from the fence. "I just wanted to say hello to Bertie. I hope you don't mind."

"That's between you and Bertie. Though I'm sure that's not quite what she had in mind for her muffins." The mare, having lost her admirers, ambled off as Jordan continued. "It's just as well you're here, anyway. I wanted to talk to you."

"About what?" Kat asked warily. The rapport had vanished, as quickly as it had come, and they were once again adversaries. The taste in her mouth had nothing to do with blueberries, everything to do with bitter regret.

"Business, what else? You didn't think it was anything personal, did you?" His tone was coolly mocking, his words sharp.

Kat sucked in a little breath. He was deliberately goading her, jabbing her just to see if it hurt. The Jordan of old had never been intentionally cruel. "Get on with it."

"I want to buy you out. I'm prepared to be very generous." He named a sum that made Kat's mouth drop open. "I want to expand the farm, and your land would give me room for more pasture. I've been thinking about this for a while."

"I'll just bet you have," Kat snapped, suddenly furious. "Since yesterday evening." She was livid. "Well, it's not for sale!"

"If you want to quibble about the price—"

"I said it's not for sale!" Kat shouted. She knew Jordan's offer wasn't just business, but a personal attack

42

meant to hurt her. And he had succeeded. She felt chagrined, mortified. "I can't believe you'd go that far just to get rid of me."

"What's so hard to understand? I need that land and I'm willing to pay for it."

"Why that particular land? Why now? No, Jordan," she said with a humorless laugh, "there's got to be more to it than that. I must be more of a thorn in your side than I thought to rate such an outrageous sum. What are you so afraid of?" She paused, considering, then continued. "It's something to think about, though. Just how high are you willing to go?"

"Name your price." Though his tone was flat, there was an element of satisfaction in his handsome face, as if, Kat thought, he'd proven something to himself.

"My price?" Suddenly, Kat began to laugh, a tight sound that bordered on hysteria. "It's more than you're willing to pay."

"Name it," he demanded.

Kat studied him, seeing the tension in his powerful body, the defiant thrust of his jaw. "All right, Jordan. My price is your forgiveness."

"What?"

"You can have everything except the house. I can't stand this enmity between us."

"You're being ridiculous."

"Why do you say that?" she demanded earnestly. "What happened to us is not so unique. Other couples break up, grow apart. And we had more reasons than most. What I felt for you then was so sweet that it makes your hatred now that much harder to take."

"Hatred?" Jordan's laugh was low and amused. "That's too strong a word. And you proved beyond a shadow of a doubt that whatever feelings you had were nothing more than cheap imitations of the real thing. No, Katherine, there's nothing left in me except indifference—and relief that I didn't make the biggest mistake of my life."

"Really? That's funny. I didn't think self-delusion was your style." Kat stepped closer, boldly placed the flat of her palm where his heart pounded in his chest. "Are you sure that's all you feel, Jordan?"

He grabbed her wrist, tightening his grip painfully until her caressing fingers peeled away. "No games, Katherine," he warned. "You'll be sorry if you try."

"I'm already sorry. I told you that." Her fingers were growing numb in his grasp but she didn't try to pull away. "Now I'm waiting for you to accept my apology."

Jordan released her then, dropping her wrist as if stung. His voice was contemptuous. "Games again! I'm not your priest. Don't come to me for absolution."

"I told you my price was high," she returned on a deep, disappointed sigh. "The Jordan I once knew was capable of paying it, though. You don't know how sorry I am to find it's beyond you now."

"Maybe it involved caring enough to make the effort," he sneered. "What makes you think you're worth it?"

"Maybe I'm not. Maybe I never was. Then again, if you want my land . . ." Kat paused and lifted her chin in challenge. "Well, Jordan? What's it going to be?"

"I don't think it will take you very long to decide to take me up on my offer," Jordan retorted, "with or without all these theatrics. When small-town life palls you'll be begging me to take that place off your hands."

"I'll starve first," Kat promised. She gave a sudden, unexpected smile, a dazzling, impish grin full of confidence. "If nothing else, just to prove you wrong."

"You're just being stubborn."

"You're right. And I'm very good at it."

He shrugged. "Suit yourself."

"I intend to," Kat said, laughing. "But get one thing

44

straight, Jordan: I'm not going anywhere! That's something you're going to have to accept whether you like it or not."

"I don't really care, Katherine," he remarked, turning back toward his car. He opened the door, then paused. "And that is something *you* must accept—like it or not."

Kat watched the car disappear up the lane and absently rubbed her wrist. "That's what you think, Jordan Scott. That's what you think!"

CHAPTER THREE

"Kat Holt! Is that really you?"

Kat dropped a head of lettuce into her shopping cart and turned toward the voice.

"Leann!"

Ignoring curious stares and the fact that their carts blocked the produce aisle, the two women hugged, pulled back, gazed at each other with delighted smiles, then hugged all over again.

"Oh, honey, don't you look super!" Leann exclaimed, beaming.

"So do you, Leann."

"Go on, now!" Leann Dickson scolded with a laugh, her plump cheeks rosy. "I know there's twenty extra pounds here somewhere. But I got them honest. I've got two daughters to prove it!"

"Two? I can't believe it," Kat cried. "You and Don?"

"Well, of course, me and Don! Who else would have me?" Leann teased. "Going on seven years now." She turned and gestured behind her. "Come here a minute, Ashlie, honey. I want you to meet one of Mama's very best friends!"

A little girl with ash-blond hair that matched her mother's short curls peered shyly from behind Leann's skirts. "Hi."

"Hi, yourself." Kat matched the little girl's smile with one of her own. "She's a doll, Leann!"

"Thanks. We left her baby sister, Leslie, at home with Don so we girls could do the shopping."

"Good idea. Oh, excuse me," Kat said, pulling her cart out of the way so another customer could get by. Leann did the same.

"You know, I heard that you were back," Leann said.

"Already?" Kat laughed, incredulous. "I only arrived the day before yesterday. I forgot how quickly word gets around in a small town."

"Word is you're home to stay," Leann probed, casually tossing tomatoes into a plastic sack. She bent and lifted Ashlie into the seat, straightening her knobby childish legs, then handing the girl a banana to amuse her.

"Then the word is right. I'm going to open up a photography studio," Kat explained.

"You are? That's great. This town could use some new blood, and a new business or two. Do you think you could take some pictures of my girls? Don and I have been meaning to have their portraits made," Leann rambled as she put sacks of potatoes and stalks of celery into the shopping cart.

"I'd be glad to any time. I'm not quite settled yet."

"You're staying at the old place?" Leann asked.

"That's right." Kat tossed a lemon into her buggy, then added an avocado.

"Have you seen Jordan yet?" Leann's voice was casual, but the look she shot Kat was sharp.

"Uh-huh." Kat rolled her eyes and grimaced.

"Like that, huh?" Leann tossed three sacks of carrots onto the rapidly growing pile in her basket.

"Yeah, like that," Kat agreed morosely.

"Gave you a hard time, did he? I'm not surprised." Leann propped a hand on her hip and drawled, "Well, whatcha goin' to do about it?" Kat's mouth dropped open

47

in surprise and she struggled to suppress a cry of sheer astonishment.

"Do? Leann, please! I haven't been home forty-eight hours and already you and Aunt Bertie are imagining things. I didn't come home to rekindle anything with Jordan Scott!"

"Didn't you?" Leann challenged skeptically.

"No, I didn't," Kat retorted, a trifle too emphatically. "Which is just as well because he's made it abundantly clear he can't stand the sight of me."

"Ah!"

"What's that supposed to mean?" Kat asked.

"Nothing," Leann replied, her cherubic face all innocence. "It's just that's not how I heard it."

"Heard what?"

"Oh, nothing. Except Don says Jordan's been as mean as a bear with a sore paw the last two days. He and Don are hunting and fishing buddies, you know. It just makes a body wonder . . ." Leann shrugged and added six cucumbers to her buggy.

"It's nothing to do with me," Kat said firmly, then hesitated. "I guess."

"Ah-ha!"

"Now don't start that again," Kat ordered fiercely before dissolving into laughter. Leann joined her, and Ashlie, not caring what the joke was, added her high peals to make it a trio.

"Whew!" Kat sighed at last when the laughter subsided. It felt wonderful to laugh again with an old friend, to let the tension drain from her body in gales of silliness. How she'd missed it! Kat wiped laugh tears from her cheeks and tried to straighten her face. "I just have one question," she told Leann.

"What's that?"

"Is all of this food for you and Don and two little girls?"

"Lord, no!" Leann giggled. "We're having a few people

over to cook out tomorrow evening. Will you come? It'll be fun and you can see some of the old crowd and meet some newcomers, too."

"Oh, Leann, that's awfully nice, but I couldn't possibly intrude."

"Piddle! We've got a lot of catching up to do. We'd love to have you. And you could even bring your camera and take some shots of the girls if you want."

"Well, if you're sure . . ."

"Positive."

Kat drove home later with directions to Leann's house and instructions to arrive early spinning in her head. She found that she was anticipating the following evening with pleasure. It would do her good to get out among other people. It had been a long time since she had indulged in something as normal as a family backyard barbecue. Deadlines, sleazy hotels, less-than-glamorous assignments in more-than-dangerous places had kept her in a rarefied atmosphere where the mundane events of everyday living took on an almost mystical appeal. A little chitchat, a charred burger, a sultry, sweaty summer evening—she could hardly wait.

Kat rounded the curve of her drive and braked suddenly. What on earth? The jungle that had been her yard had almost completely disappeared as if by magic. Men mowed, raked, chopped weeds, and bundled up trash in a veritable flurry of activity. Before her eyes a real yard appeared, complete with neatly trimmed shrubbery and a manicured lawn. Kat stumbled out of the car and headed for the nearest worker, a man pushing a lawnmower.

"Hey, what's going on?" she demanded. "Who are you people?"

"Evening, miss," the man said, doffing his baseball cap and wiping his sweat-dewed forehead. "We're the crew from Scott Farms."

"What?" Kat couldn't believe her ears. "I didn't arrange for any of this! Who sent you?"

"Dunno, now that I think about it," he said, jamming his cap back on. "We just had orders to come help with the yard work. Nearly done, now. How do you like it?"

"Oh, it's very nice," Kat hastened to tell him. "In fact, I can hardly believe my eyes!"

"We're just finishing up. Shouldn't be too hard to keep now. Well, I'll get back to it, miss," he said, then headed the mower down another strip of grass while Kat looked on in complete astonishment.

Had Jordan sent his men to clean up the yard? Impossible. Why would he do a thing like that? Maybe Aunt Bertie had sent them without Jordan's knowledge. That had to be it, Kat decided, retrieving her purchases from the car. She grabbed the wire handle of a paint pail and lugged it to the porch, heaving the gallon of black paint onto the steps. She left it there and went back for her single sack of groceries. She would have to thank Bertie for the help.

She set the sack on the kitchen table and began to unload it. Cheese, apples, a lemon, a loaf of wheat bread—her hands hesitated as a thought struck her. What if Bertie wasn't responsible? Was Jordan trying to sweeten her up with a show of neighborly concern so he could slip in under her defenses? He probably considered it a good investment to get the property cleaned up since he fully expected her to sell it to him shortly. How like him to try to take control! She should have realized his reasoning would be devious and calculating.

Kat made a little sound of disgust as she realized she was squeezing the hapless loaf of bread. Better it should be Jordan's neck, she thought as she put the bread away. Who did he think he was? Well, she'd certainly have a thing or two to tell him the next time their paths crossed.

They crossed exactly twenty-four hours later.

Kat sat cross-legged on the thick saint augustine grass at

50

the edge of the patio behind the Dicksons' modest brick home, watching Ashlie and Leslie play with a gray kitten. Her camera shutter clicked furiously, catching the girls' unselfconscious smiles and childish squeals of delight. The natural, familiar setting made a backdrop that allowed the two little girls to respond spontaneously. She couldn't have asked for more precious subjects and she knew instinctively that she was capturing just what two doting parents would adore. It was a thrilling experience, and Kat couldn't wait to see the results of the shoot.

She got to her feet, dusting off her khaki pants and matching camp shirt, then crouched slightly, too intent on her subjects to notice the other guests arriving. Leslie squealed delightedly, then raised her chubby arms, her angelic, toothless smile widening. Suddenly Kat found herself looking at Jordan through her camera. He lifted the child and his muscular shoulders flexed under the royal blue knit shirt he wore. Automatically, with the artist's eye, Kat continued to snap the shutter, capturing his lean, handsome face smiling down at the wispy-haired infant, a look of indulgence on his face when Leslie examined his straight teeth with her fingers, patted his cheeks, then gave him a slobbery, open-mouthed baby kiss.

Kat caught it all, seeing snatches of things through the viewfinder that stirred her, tormented her, damned her. He was a man capable of great love and the tenderest passion, she well knew, yet he hid it under a reserved, cynical façade. Why was he content to lavish his affection on other people's children? Had her betrayal and rejection scarred him so badly that he could never trust another woman? Was that why he was still alone? Or, and Kat's heart beat faster at the thought, was it something more than that? Something so elemental that it was fruitless to search for another love, as if in all the world Jordan and Kat were the only ones meant for each other, like two pieces of a puzzle that made no sense until they were joined to reveal the

51

true, beautiful picture. It was a dangerous, thrilling fantasy.

Kat lowered her camera as well as her defenses, and watched Jordan with all the naked longing in her heart revealed in her expression. His attention had been riveted on the child but he felt her gaze, and their eyes met in the instant before she shuttered her expression again. His lips parted and he drew in a harsh breath, his brown eyes golden in the soft evening light.

"Are you all through with my midgets?" Leann asked, coming up behind Kat. "It's past their bedtime."

Kat whirled and forced herself to smile brightly. "Of course. They were angels, Leann. I'm sure we've got something you'll like."

"Oh, great! But now it's time for you to enjoy yourself. You didn't come to work all night, after all." Leann scooped up her offspring, one under each arm. "I'll be right back. Get Kat a drink, will you, Jordan?" she said over her shoulder before walking toward the house.

"What would you like, Katherine?" Jordan asked.

For him to touch her, just once, like he used to, Kat thought in momentary anguish.

She swallowed and forced herself to concentrate on the simple act of replacing her lens cap. At that moment it seemed an insurmountable task. Finally, the flat black disk snapped over the lens. She lifted a composed face, her flight of fancy grounded in reality once again.

"Don't bother, Jordan. I can get it myself."

"I don't care to buck one of Leann's direct orders," he answered, his lips twisting. His fingers lightly cupped her elbow and he tugged her toward a makeshift bar at one end of the patio. "A beer? A little wine?"

"Wine, please." Kat struggled to still the inner tremors at his touch. She slipped free of his grasp with the excuse of replacing the camera in its case and setting it safely aside. When she returned, Jordan was holding a glass toward her, and thankfully, Don Dickson was engaging him in conversation.

Kat sipped the crisp Chablis slowly, allowing the liquid to trickle down her dry throat and hoping the alcohol would relax the tense muscles in her neck. She didn't know why she was surprised to find Jordan there, but she hadn't been prepared for it. There was nothing more humiliating than throwing herself at a man who didn't want her. The thought that Jordan had seen her unguarded expression caused a fiery heat to rise up her neck. She longed to escape, but at that moment Leann reappeared with an entourage of guests, and Kat was quickly caught up in saying hello to people she hadn't seen in years.

As something of a local celebrity, Kat was instantly surrounded by a crowd of friends all asking questions about her career, her travels, and the famous people she had met. She kept her audience entertained with amusing anecdotes, laughingly responding to their queries, but she was always conscious of Jordan's eyes resting on her.

"Ain't it great to have Kat back home again?" Don asked the group in general. His slightly balding pate glistened with moisture from the heat of the evening and the fire in the barbecue pit he was tending. His waist, thickened by a few extra pounds over the years, was covered with a bright yellow-checked apron that proclaimed "Equal Opportunity Kitchen." He grabbed Kat around the waist and gave her a friendly squeeze. "We'll just have to make this a kind of welcome home party tonight."

"Thanks, Don," Kat said. "It's good to be back."

Don took a pull on his long-necked beer and leered pointedly at Jordan. "Well, what do you say, man? Ain't it great?"

"Great." Jordan's laconic reply was lost amid casual chatter of conversation, but Kat's ears were finely attuned to catch his sardonic inflection.

"As soon as I get these steaks cooked, we'll get down to

53

some serious partying," Don promised, releasing Kat to stir the coals in the barbecue grill. "Gosh, I guess the last time we were all together was—when was that? Must've been your birthday party, Kat, remember? The summer after you and Leann graduated. Lord, we danced all night! Don't know how your grandpa stood us. You remember, don't you, Jordan?"

"I remember." Jordan's tawny gaze fastened on Kat's blazing countenance. She hastily swallowed the rest of her wine to cover her discomfort.

"Come to think of it, you left early that night, didn't you?" Don asked his friend. Leann chose that moment to shove a tray of T-bones into Don's stomach, causing her husband to give a startled grunt.

"When are you going to learn to button that lip of yours?" Leann hissed under her breath. Then louder, ignoring her husband's puzzled look of protest, "You get those steaks on, Don Dickson, or we'll never eat supper tonight. Come on, Kat. I need some help in the kitchen." She hauled Kat unceremoniously out of the crowd and into the house.

"Thanks, Leann," Kat said as they entered the spacious kitchen.

"Honestly, sometimes that man acts like he hasn't got the brains God gave an armadillo! But he's got a hide like one! Insensitive, crass—"

In spite of herself Kat began to laugh. "He didn't mean anything by it, Leann."

"I know, but . . ." She gave a sigh of exasperation as she checked on potatoes baking in the oven. "That was the night you and Jordan broke up for good, wasn't it?"

"Yes." Kat touched her friend's arm. "I'm all right. Don't worry about it. Did you really need some help?"

"Sure. Here, slice these cucumbers, will you?"

Kat picked up a knife and fell to with a will. The mundane task helped to calm her jangled nerves. Soon the smell of sizzling beef lay tantalizingly on the evening air and Don hollered that everything was ready.

Kat helped Leann carry out platters of golden corn on the cob, baked potatoes, pungent garlic bread, and a huge bowl of salad. A short time later everyone was sitting around the patio, on the lawn, in the old-fashioned swing hanging beneath the tall oak tree, anywhere a seat could be found, with their paper plates sagging under the weight of the food. The sun was down, cooling the evening considerably, and soft music echoed from the stereo speakers on the patio.

Kat's appetite was not up to the effort to consume even half of what was offered her, but she made a valiant effort, then went to dump the remains in the garbage sack Leann had provided. Jordan and Don sat nearby, their elbows propped on their knees, making inroads into large ears of corn dripping with butter. Kat thought they both had an endearing boyish quality to them as they ate with gusto. She found it hard to tear her eyes away from Jordan's strong white teeth sinking into the pale kernels. Abruptly, she tossed her plate away. It would be better for everyone, especially herself, if she made an early night of it. She paused, scanning the yard for Leann so she could thank her and leave.

"Still haven't found another hand to work the horses?" Don asked Jordan.

"Nobody I can trust," Jordan replied, tossing the empty cob into the plate in his lap and wiping his hands with a paper napkin. "If you hear of anyone who needs the job, let me know. I could sure use the help. We've had an influx of mares to breed and I'm fast running out of paddock area, too. Don't know what I'm going to do about that."

"Maybe Kat could help you out," Don suggested, dragging Kat into the conversation with a gesture. "Your place runs with Scott Farms. Maybe you could lease him your pastures or something."

"I've already thought of that," Jordan admitted, standing up. He held his empty plate easily in one hand and dangled his beer bottle from the other. "You've had some time to think about it, Katherine. Are you going to accept my offer?"

Kat's mouth tightened. She was irritated that Jordan would put her on the spot in front of Don. "Are you going to accept mine?" she returned, her voice challenging.

"What offer is that?" Don asked around a mouthful of corn.

"Oh, nothing. Just a little business proposition. Katherine's not too keen on it, but I'm sure she'll come around in time," Jordan replied.

"Don't bet your life savings on it," Kat snapped. "And by the way, who gave you permission to have those men of yours clean up my yard?"

"I thought they did a pretty good job. Weren't you satisfied?" Jordan's voice was deceptively mild.

"That's not the problem and you know it!"

"Excuse us, Don," Jordan said, tossing the remains of his meal away. "Kat and I need to get this hashed out."

"Sure, sure," Don said, waving his fork like a sword. "Don't run off, though. Leann's got dessert coming soon."

Before Kat could protest, the insistent pressure of Jordan's hand on her arm led her to a secluded corner of the yard under the graceful branches of a weeping willow tree. A pale full moon hung saucerlike in the darkness and shadows moved eerily in the corner away from the brightly lit patio.

"Will you let go?" Kat demanded, snatching her arm away. "We have got absolutely nothing to hash out."

"I'm prepared to double my offer on your land. I need it badly, and I just don't want it lying there unused when you decide to take off again."

"You're beginning to sound like a broken record, Jordan. I wish you'd get it through your thick skull that I'm not going anywhere!"

"Then what are you so irate about?"

"Irate? I'll show you irate! You can take your double offer, quadruple it, then run it up the flag pole and salute it for all I care." She glared up into his shadowed face. "And keep your crew out of my yard!"

"Did it ever occur to you I was just trying to help you out?"

"Don't do me any favors! I'll let the grass grow up sky high if I want. So don't go taking liberties where you have no right."

"Liberties?" His voice was low and angry. "Stick around, Katherine, and those aren't the only kinds of liberties I'm liable to take!"

Stunned, Kat could find no retort to his words. They stared at each other, breaths suddenly erratic, hearts beating out of control. The pale green fronds of the willow stirred softly on the breeze and the sounds of music and laughter from the patio seemed to recede, enclosing them in a bubble of intimacy.

Jordan's eyes dropped, scanned Kat from the hollow of her throat revealed by the notched collar of her shirt, down over the indentation of her waist and her long legs. Kat's skin tingled as though he had touched her, sliding a warm callused palm across every sensitive nerve ending. She licked her dry lips and touched the gold loop dangling from her ear.

"Am I making you nervous, Katherine?" Jordan asked softly, stepping closer so that she could almost feel the warmth of his body. She shook her head in wordless denial and he chuckled. "I could always tell when you were worried or nervous because you played with your earrings."

Kat's hand dropped away from her ear like a shot. "Jordan . . ."

"You're making me more than nervous, Kat," he admitted. "You're making me crazy."

"Don't, Jordan," she said weakly.

"Why did you have to come back? Was it just to torment me?"

"No," she whispered, "only myself." Her heart hammered in triple time and a strange lethargy stole through her limbs. He loomed over her, so close she could smell the tangy scent of his cologne, yet she was powerless to move away.

If he touched her, he'd be done for, Jordan warned himself, closing his eyes momentarily against the moonlit beauty of her face, the troubled, smoky blue depths of her eyes.

She wished he would touch her, just for a minute to ease the ache.

"It's not going to work, is it?" he muttered, shaking his head slightly. "You and me in the same town. It's not going to work."

"No." Kat swallowed and dipped her head in acknowledgment. Resignation and disappointment mixed within her.

"What are we going to do about it?" he rumbled.

"Nothing. Nothing at all." Her voice was barely a whisper. She turned away, intent only on escape. His large, warm hands caught her shoulders, stilling her flight and tugging her inexorably back. Kat was surprised to feel tremors in his fingers. "Stop, Jordan," she begged, suddenly panicky. She pulled away, fighting him like a frightened bird caught in a fowling net. "This isn't what you want!"

"The hell it's not," he whispered hoarsely. He pulled her to him, and she fell full length against the hard, muscular planes of his body, her hands caught between them. With a low moan he lowered his mouth and captured her lips.

Kat was all he remembered—and more. Sexy, womanly, as mysterious as Eve. He was ravenous, starving for the taste of her, and he hadn't even known it. Jordan brushed his mouth against Kat's, probing sensuously with the tip of his tongue until her lips parted, allowing him freedom to explore at will. A feeling of triumph surged through him as he plunged within the sweet, dark recesses of her mouth. He cupped the back of her head, threading his fingers through the soft silkiness of her hair to hold her still, but she didn't resist him.

It was odd how one's will to resist vanished just when one needed it most, Kat mused, dazed. She had expected a brutal, punishing assault in keeping with Jordan's hostility, yet this kiss was no means of revenge. It was the kiss she had felt only in her dreams, the one she'd awakened from with tears in her eyes because it had been only a dream. And now . . . now . . . Her hands slowly slid up to Jordan's neck and she pressed her breasts against his chest. Her fingers smoothed the thick burnished hair on the sides of his head, and, daringly, she met his tongue with her own.

Her tongue dueling with his in an electric ritual that sparked through his body surprised Jordan. He tightened his arms around her and she fit to him perfectly, every inch of her just made to please only him. His hand slid to her hip, cupped her firm buttock, settled her intimately against him. He felt the answering pressure of her pelvis and groaned into her mouth.

He lifted his lips from hers, moving away only the space of a breath, a breath that mingled erratically between them as a single sigh.

"Why do you have to wear these damn pants?" he murmured, his palm massaging her bottom. "I hate to see you cover up your gorgeous legs."

"You always liked me best in a skirt." Her words were tremulous.

"I always liked you best in nothing at all."

Kat's sigh was almost a moan. Desire flared between them, so insistent that all was forgotten, the past, the future, even the present and the fact that they stood in a crowded backyard in the shadow of a willow tree.

"I wish to God I knew what to do about you," he said huskily. She heard his harsh swallow, felt his subtle withdrawal even before his hands came up to ease her clasp around his neck.

"Do?" she echoed. They stood separate again, and the loss of his touch was a tangible pain.

"Should I throw you down on the Dicksons' lawn and make love to you just to get you out of my system, or ride you out of town on a rail?"

"I wouldn't advise you try either one." Her breath caught in her throat as she battled for composure. "Not if you value your hide."

"Oh, my hide's tough enough. But you did a number on my heart a long time ago. I don't think I care to risk it again."

"No one asked you to," Kat argued.

"Then what are you asking, Katherine?" His voice was suddenly mocking and cynical. "Is it an affair you want? No strings, no ties, just unadulterated sex and plenty of it? I think I can oblige."

"Stop it!"

"Does the truth hurt?"

"You wouldn't know the truth if it slapped you in the face."

From across the yard, Don called them, promising cake and ice cream in return for an appearance. Grateful for the interruption, Kat edged away, but Jordan caught her wrist.

"Shall we?" he goaded.

Kat snatched her hand back. "Just leave me alone, Jordan. Leave me alone."

"I suppose cake and ice cream are too much to resist,

especially for a girl who likes birthday parties as well as you," he taunted.

Kat's eyes blazed like blue flames. She stood stiff and proud, her gaze direct. "I wouldn't know, since my last birthday party was eleven years ago."

Her final words were low, a challenge to Jordan to make of them what he would, "I haven't had anything to celebrate since then."

CHAPTER FOUR

It was no good. She couldn't sleep.

Kat threw back the rumpled sheet and sat up, running a shaky hand through her hair. The old iron bedstead that had once been Papa John's rattled and squeaked, its springs protesting. The pale ray of moonlight streamed in through the open window. Not a breath of air stirred.

Kat sighed, blotting the faint sheen of moisture from her forehead with the back of her hand. She stood abruptly and went to lean on the windowsill, gazing out through the screen. She could see the grove of pines clearly, tall silhouettes illuminated by the cool lunar light. A strange restlessness filled her.

What was the matter with her? she chided herself. But she knew what was wrong. It could be summed up in two words: Jordan Scott.

After her disastrous conversation with Jordan, Kat couldn't leave the Dicksons' party quickly enough. But now, in the privacy of her own home, she knew she had made a mistake. At least at the party there had been other people to talk to, other things to occupy her thoughts. Here, she was alone, with only memories of that brief, inflaming kiss to keep her company.

And at the thought her traitorous body betrayed her anew, her nipples tightened, so sensitive that even the thin silk of the shapeless nightshirt she wore was too abrasive on the tender, aching buds. With a muttered exclamation, Kat crossed her arms over her breasts and leaned against the window casing. She breathed shallowly and tried to ignore the demands of her body.

Despite what Jordan had suggested, she wasn't just looking for sexual release. Although a part of her ached, it was much more than that. It was the age-old need to love and be loved, to share the little things with someone who understood, the desire to put loneliness behind her forever. Kat sighed. Maybe returning home *had* been a mistake. Because home had changed, and she had changed, everything had changed except Jordan's enmity. A bitter anger welled suddenly in her heart, a rage against fate and Rosalind Scott's manipulations and Jordan's stubborn, unforgiving streak.

Kat watched the fluttering patches of light and shadow under the trees and heard the mournful whistle of a distant whippoorwill. Memories of other quiet moonlit nights rushed over her, fleeting pictures of lovers' tender meetings, softly spoken confidences, passionate embraces. How many times had she slipped quietly from the house to meet Jordan in their secret place? The conflict between their families had made traditional dating almost impossible, for being together gave birth to malicious gossip and recriminations at home. So they had sought their privacy in the solitude of the woods beside the swimming hole where they'd played and splashed as kids.

What had Jordan said? He'd like to get her out of his system. Well, so would she! Kat straightened, pressed her warm cheek against the cool metal mesh of the window screen. She'd like to get on with her life, to answer Jordan's coolness with iciness of her own. But how could she when everything she saw reminded her of him and the love they had shared? The ardent young man he'd once been haunted her, hounded her like a demon intent on snaring her soul. How could she exorcise him and free herself of the tenacious memories and longings?

To begin, she decided, she had to accept that however much they still attracted each other, Jordan would never forgive her, never feel anything for her other than contempt. If she could understand that one fact, then maybe her crazy heart wouldn't drum every time she saw him. She pushed away from the window, her hands moving restlessly. Maybe the only way was to confront the ghosts of their past head on. Her resolve formed, took shape. That something she could do now, on this moonlit night.

Kat slipped her feet into flat sandals, then made her way through the dark, silent little house, out through the back door into the silvery moonlight. Crickets chirped, their noisy racket pausing momentarily as she moved through the grass, then returning with renewed vigor. The white silk of her large nightshirt glittered under the moon's cool rays, the hem rustling sensually against her bare thighs. Dew gathered on her toes, but Kat ignored the moisture, intent on picking her way down the well-remembered path, past the path that led to Scott Farms, further into the woods toward the gentle sounds of trickling water.

She found the clearing and paused, shocked that it could have remained so unchanged even after all these years. The moon trailed in glimmering streaks across the little pool whose sandy edges looked almost golden. The old deformed sweet gum stood where it always had, its L-shape forming a natural platform perfect for diving or sitting hand in hand. How many times had she and Jordan sat there, their legs swinging, laughing together, whispering lovers' secrets?

Kat walked slowly to the tree, then touched the rough bark almost reverently. Her fingers trailed across the wide bole, then upward on the stem of the L. Without thought, she climbed into the crook of the tree, sitting as she always had, feet swinging free, one arm wrapped for balance around the upthrust portion of the trunk. The uneven texture of the bark dug into her thighs and bottom, but she ignored the discomfort, overcome by memory.

Against the darker shapes of brush and trees, the cool phosphorescent light of a firefly flickered on and off, a love signal to a distant mate. The answer came and to Kat they looked like sparks floating upward through the night from a glowing fire. Memory overtook her and Kat stared sightlessly, seeing the small campfire, the bend of Jordan's bare back as he tended it, the flash of a white grin cast over his shoulder at something she'd said. A poignancy so sweet it hurt rushed through Kat and unconsciously her fingers dug into the bark of the tree. Golden firelight illuminated his strong features, and the undeniable tenderness in his golden brown eyes had changed to desire.

With a groan, Kat dropped her forehead against the tree. She'd been mad to come here. This was no exorcism; this was torture! She heaved a great sigh, then felt the hairs on the back of her neck quiver inexplicably. Some sixth sense made her look up. Her breath stopped in her throat.

Jordan watched her from across the clearing, his dark hair tousled, his white shirt hanging unbuttoned to reveal the curly hair on his chest, his features inscrutable in the silvery light. He stood poised, waiting, the powerful muscles of his thighs straining against the faded denim of his jeans. Involuntarily, Kat shuddered. Had she conjured him up out of her imagination, a figment of her own longing?

"I knew you'd come." His voice was husky, mesmerizing, but very real. Kat's momentary relief was instantly replaced by a new tension.

"You did?" Her whisper was tremulous, confused.

Jordan didn't know what had brought him through the night to her, but he'd been drawn surely as iron filings find a magnet. He cursed this folly, but in the clingy thing she wore she was like a white-hot flame and he the moth circling frantically, drawn against his will to his own destruction.

He moved forward slowly, his golden brown eyes never leaving her face. When he stood in front of her he paused, gazing down at her with a ferocious expression marring his handsome features. Kat's blood roared in her ears and she swallowed harshly on a thrill of fear. Jordan's hands reached out, touched the tops of her shoulders, slipping under the boat neckline of her shirt for a minute before splaying out around the slim column of her neck.

"Damn you," he muttered hoarsely. "You're like a poison in my blood."

"Don't, Jordan." Her heart fluttered deep in her breast.

"I can't help myself."

Kat's fingers curled around his wrists. His dark head bent, and she felt his lips on the side of her neck. Her eyelids fluttered down and her breathing checked, then rushed outward in a series of little panting sighs. He opened his mouth against her skin, breathing in her night-warmed scent that smelled like the finest perfume. Then with the edge of his teeth he gently nipped the cord of her neck, sending shivers down her spine to lodge low in her belly. His tongue flicked out, testing the texture of her skin, and Kat felt the air falling cool on the wet trail he left. She moaned softly.

"Do you remember, Kat? How good it was?" His lips left a trail of fire across her collarbone, then dipped to stroke the small raised scar on her shoulder. His thumbs lightly massaged the tender hollows behind her ears.

"Yes, I remember." She arched her neck sensuously, and her low laugh was shaky. The silver-mottled darkness gave her courage, gave her the ability to say things she couldn't have in the light of day. "How could I forget?"

"There could have been others." Jordan drew back, his eyes darkening.

"Not for a long while," she admitted honestly. "It's never been like it was between the two of us. Never."

Jordan felt a surge of something akin to pleasure at her softly spoken words, but a niggling jealousy forced him to ask, "Your partner?"

"Bill?" She frowned, trying to force the sadness away. "Not Bill. We were friends. I miss him. I don't want to talk about it."

"All right." He acquiesced without pushing further. He continued to hold her shoulders and felt her fingers tremble on his wrists.

"What—what do you want, Jordan?" she faltered.

"I don't know. One minute I want to hurt you as much as you hurt me, the next . . ."

"What?"

Her breathy prompting warmed his cheek. "I want to be inside you," he growled. "To feel you around me, to love you until we're both sobbing with the joy of it."

Sudden moisture gleamed in her eyes. "Is that possible?"

"God help me, I don't know." He released her and pulled away, turning his back and running a troubled hand through his tangled hair. "I wish you'd never come home, Kat."

"Yes, I know."

Kat watched him walk toward the edge of the water, his broad shoulders bent, his fists jammed into his pockets. The moon's reflection glistened on the tips of his hair and suddenly she couldn't stand the distance between them. She climbed carefully down and went to stand beside him. She picked up a smooth pebble and tossed it in, sending shimmering ripples across the water.

"Remember," she began, "remember the time we came turtle hunting?"

"Yeah." He chuckled. "We were going to sell them and

67

make enough to buy a bus ticket to Houston to see the Astros play."

"*You* were. *I* wanted a pair of roller skates."

"We didn't have much luck, as I recall."

"You fell in."

"*You* pushed me," he clarified. "Did you ever get those skates?"

She smiled and shook her head. "But it was worth it just to see you splutter. That was during your insufferable period, I think."

"Me?" He snorted disbelievingly. "I was always a model of decorum."

"Ha! You were a snotty Washington brat. And you loved making my life miserable whenever you came home."

"That's because you always went off like a firecracker at the least little thing."

"I don't call putting worms in my underwear a little thing!" she said indignantly, but tried not to laugh.

"Ah, but you got me back," he said solemnly.

"I did? How?"

"You grew up." He turned to gaze at her, his eyes singeing the bare flesh of her thighs, the rounded mounds of her breasts under the light silk, the sultry curve of her mouth.

Kat licked her suddenly dry lips. "We both did."

"I remember the night Lady Sabrina's Dream was born. We were both so high with excitement and so proud of ourselves there was no getting us to go home, so we came here."

"We were friends then . . . best friends," she murmured.

"That night was the first time I knew I wanted you," Jordan said softly.

"It was?" Kat felt surprised. "But that was . . ." Her mind raced. "Two years before . . ."

"Yes. I had to wait for you to grow up. You didn't disappoint me."

"Jordan! I had no idea." Inside Kat's chest a weight seemed to grow unbearably heavy. She had not guessed the depth of his devotion then. It made what she had had to do even more distressing. How would she ever make it up to him? Could she? Hesitantly, she reached out, her fingers lightly touching his muscular chest, the soft dark hairs that tapered down to disappear beneath his belt buckle.

"Stop it!" he ground out, jerking her hand away. "There's no quick fix for what happened. I wouldn't want it anyway."

Chagrined, Kat blushed. "It's not that. I just wanted to . . . to . . ." She couldn't express her need to touch him, to try to somehow convey all that she was feeling to him.

"To what, Kat?" The hand that pushed her away suddenly pulled her forward against his chest. His arm tightened across her back, flattening her breasts against him. "Is this what you want?" he asked, insolently running a hand up her side. He cupped her breast so firmly she was nearly lifted off her feet.

Kat gasped, raising her stunned face to Jordan. She squirmed against his arrogant expression, but he held her firmly.

"Let go," she demanded, pushing against his shoulders.

"Is this what you came home for?" he asked, grinding his hips intimately against hers, letting her feel his desire.

"Jordan, please." Kat's breathing faltered and her heart thumped painfully in her chest.

"By God, it might be the only way to make sure you leave," he muttered harshly.

Kat opened her mouth to protest, but his lips covered hers in a hot, demanding kiss that sent her senses reeling. His tongue plunged savagely into her mouth, twining with her tongue in a fiery possession. There was nothing gentle in him now. He was all male, dominant, intent on taking everything she had.

His hands roamed up and down her spine, savored the

outline of her hip. The smooth silk of her shirt rustled against her skin, the rough texture of his palms catching the delicate material. Suddenly, he lifted her, and without releasing her mouth walked to the bent tree and set her upon it. Kat felt the rough rasp of bark against her tender skin and the black desire that stormed through Jordan. Everything that tormented him seemed to have loosed its hold, breaking through his normal restraints and releasing all the pent-up anger and hurt in a maelstrom of passion.

Kat felt as though her lungs would burst, as if he sucked all the oxygen from her body with his punishing, bruising kisses. Incredibly, they were unbelievably erotic, arousing in her an answering need. He sapped every bit of will from her with his overpowering demands, and whether it was the will to resist or the will to respond she didn't know. Kat whimpered helplessly.

Instantly, Jordan's mouth softened to soothe, to elicit a response she couldn't deny. His fingers threaded through her hair to cup the back of her head. He pushed her until her spine rested against the back of the natural chair and her hands came up to balance on his shoulders. Releasing her mouth, he dropped kisses across her eyelids, down her nose, pausing ever so slightly on the tiny uneven bump in its center, then nibbling along the side of her jaw.

Kat sucked in great drafts of air, her eyes glazed. Jordan's fingers caressed her breast, and he rotated the pad of his thumb against the swollen, turgid nipple. Kat cried out, but he moved closer, lifting one of her legs behind the sensitive knee and swinging it over the tree trunk so that she straddled the log. He swung his leg over, then leaned against her, seeking her lips again in a series of long, drugging kisses.

His hands moved knowingly over her, touching her everywhere. He slipped under the hem of the nightshirt to discover the warmth and smoothness of her belly, her breasts, her back. Then he traveled over the brief triangle of silk at the apex of her thighs, cupping the fount of her femininity and gently massaging.

Kat clutched Jordan's neck and shuddered convulsively. "Rusty!" she cried. "Oh, God! Rusty!"

Jordan recoiled as if he'd been shot, but Kat, not understanding, clung to his neck. He reached up and pulled her hands free, breathing hard. He lurched away, staggering to his feet.

Jordan felt sick with self-loathing. His hands trembled. He was aghast at the unleashed violence of his actions. He had never treated a woman like that, never! Yet he'd made love to Kat to punish her, to make her hate him so that she'd have no choice but to get out of his life. At least that's what he had intended at first. But things had changed. She was sweet, and as giving as he remembered. He'd reached for the two-edged sword of revenge and he'd been the one to be pierced. He'd wanted her, yes, but at the end it had been not out of hate, but with all the tenderness of the past. And then she'd called him Rusty, the name she'd used in love, in teasing, in laughter, and suddenly the ugly mockery and sham of what he did shattered him. Jordan ran a shaking hand down his jaw. Oh, God, what was happening to him?

Confused, and feeling as though she would explode at any second, Kat struggled to understand what was happening to her. Humiliation sizzled through her. He had done this just to drive her away! To prove to himself she was the wanton, irresponsible female he thought she was. He had tried to use her responses against her in a degrading surrender. And like a fool, she had let him! She hastily adjusted her shirt and swung herself to a sitting position, then buried her humiliated, flaming face in her hands, willing herself not to cry.

"Did I hurt you?" Jordan asked hoarsely.

"What do you think?" she replied bitterly, her voice muffled by her hands.

71

Jordan wheeled around and squatted down beside her. "I'm sorry. God, I'm sorry. I didn't mean—" He broke off, his jaw working. "I told you not to stay, Kat. If you do I'll hurt you again."

"Go away."

"Don't make me hurt you, Kat," he almost begged. She refused to lift her head.

"Just go away, please."

She heard his tired sigh, heard the crunch of sticks and underbrush as he stood. Briefly, she thought she felt the light pressure of his hand on her hair.

"I won't bother you again," he said painfully. "Are you going to be all right?"

Slowly, Kat straightened to gaze accusingly at him. "I'm no worse than I was."

Jordan winced and in that instant Kat forgot her humiliation to wonder at the source of the raw pain in his eyes.

"I'll walk you home."

"I'm not afraid of the dark," she said.

"But—"

"No. Please." Her voice quavered and she bit her lip. She heard him take another shaky breath.

"All right, Kat. You win."

He turned away, strode to the edge of the clearing and paused as if he would say something, but didn't. He disappeared into the enveloping darkness. Kat followed him with her eyes until his white shirt blended into the forest and vanished completely.

Only then did she climb down from the tree. Her legs felt weak and she swayed drunkenly, then steadied. Still she gazed after Jordan, puzzled and distressed by what had just happened between them. He hadn't meant to hurt her, she decided at last, although to bring her to fever pitch then reject her so callously had done just that. His emotions had always run deep though he tried to suppress them, showing only a calm exterior to the outside world. At

72

one time, she had known him better than anyone and could understand his moods, his needs. Maybe she still did. She knew that whatever he did, she was the one who had driven him to it. A tiny flicker of hope came alive in her heart. Had his sudden remorse indicated a deeper emotion? Everyone knew there was a thin line between love and hate. Did he still care for her?

Please God, let it be so, she prayed silently. Because only then would she ever have a chance for happiness. In those few moments between the fire of Jordan's dark possession and his cold rejection, she had known again the glory and sweetness of their coming together.

And now she realized that she still loved Jordan Scott, had never stopped loving him, and wanted him back with all her heart.

CHAPTER FIVE

It was wonderful to discover she was in love, but terrible to realize she didn't know what to do about it, Kat thought. What could she do when the man in question had vowed not to bother her again and seemed damned determined to carry out that ridiculous promise? In the week and a half since she'd last seen Jordan, there had been ample opportunity for Kat to wrestle with the problem. How was a woman going to win her man's heart and trust again if she never saw him?

Kat fiddled with the f-stop on her Rolleiflex and tried to concentrate on the job at hand. "All right, everyone, here we go," she announced.

The flash went off, capturing the happy faces of the bride and groom and their entire wedding party. Kat rapidly lined up the next series of poses, arranging the couple's hands over the bride's bouquet for a traditional shot of the wedding rings.

"Hold it," she warned, then clicked the shutter again.

A quirk of fate, a minor auto accident, the last-minute rush to locate a replacement photographer, and suddenly Kat had a job. And a very prestigious one at that—the wedding of the season between the daughter of one of Mansfield's founding families and the good-looking football player she had met at LSU. Kat framed their beaming faces in the viewfinder and snapped again.

They were just children, she thought, focusing carefully on the young bride's blushing countenance. They looked so happy, but what did they really know about love? Not enough, Kat was certain, but maybe that was a good thing. She silently wished them luck.

"Just one more shot," she promised with a smile, "then you can start enjoying your party."

The bride and groom laughed together and gazed soulfully into each other's eyes. *Perfect*, Kat thought, and snapped the picture. Minutes later she roamed around the spacious Fellowship Hall taking candid shots of the attendants and wedding guests enjoying the lavish reception. Everyone who was anyone in Mansfield was there.

"How's it going, Miss Photographer?"

Kat grinned and snapped a picture of Leann, who looked rather smashing in a linen suit and wide-brimmed hat. "Just fine! And thanks for steering the McElroys my way. I'm sure this is the break I've been waiting for."

"Hey, you're welcome. They were glad to find someone with your credentials on such short notice. It takes time to build a clientele, so don't get discouraged."

"I'm trying, but it's hard with so much free time on my hands. I've even thought about looking for a studio job in Shreveport."

"Don't give up yet," Leann urged. "After everyone sees what a marvelous job you do on this wedding, I'm sure word will get around."

"Ever an optimist!" Kat teased. "Didn't you let Don come with you today?"

"I'll give you one guess where he is." Leann laughed, pointing toward the crowded buffet tables. "He said he was going to check out the grazing. Uh-oh."

"Uh-oh, what?" Kat asked.

"Look who just walked in." Leann nodded in the direction of the door. Kat followed her glance and felt her heart sink.

Jordan, looking incredibly handsome in a dark tailored suit, paused at the door with his companion, a devastatingly pretty woman with a fluff of strawberry curls. His eyes flicked over the room and hesitated on the two women. With purposeful steps he crossed the crowded room toward them.

"Don't worry about this one," Leann said under her breath to Kat. She hid a tiny grin before Jordan and his date bore down on them. "She's a zero upstairs."

But Kat wasn't so sure if that made any difference to a man, for the woman was a feminine froth, all ruffles and softness and peachy complexion and eyes filled with melting vulnerability and adoration as she gazed at Jordan. Kat felt suddenly plain in her silk shantung sheath with its large buttons down the back, even though when she put it on she had thought it had just the right touch of professional elegance. The aqua dress she'd picked up at a Parisian designer's closeout skimmed her slim figure, hinting, but never blatantly revealing, and the high heels she wore accentuated the delicacy of her ankles and shapely turn of her calves.

"Well, hello!" Leann bubbled, her eyes sparkling with mischief. "Jordan and Sondra, how nice! Isn't this a wonderful reception?"

"Very nice." Jordan smiled at Leann, but favored Kat with only a laconic nod. He did, however, make a point of introducing her to Sondra, and Kat began to seethe. He was doing this deliberately, sending her signals loud and clear, escorting a beautiful woman to prove that he had no interest in Kat. Impishly, Kat decided that two could play at the game.

"You certainly make a lovely couple," she cooed brightly. "Let me take a few shots of you."

Sondra immediately cuddled up to Jordan, sliding her hand through his arm and preening. "Oh, is my hair all right? Maybe I should put on some more lipstick?"

"No, you're perfect," Kat assured her, backing up slightly to focus the camera. "Now smile!"

Sondra batted her overmascaraed lashes and simpered, clinging to Jordan's arm.

"That's right, Jordan," Kat encouraged maliciously. "Go ahead and put your arms around her." She suppressed a giggle at the dark ruddy wave of color that began to spread up Jordan's neck. She clicked shot after shot.

Finally, Jordan called a halt. "That's enough," he said, smiling tightly at Sondra.

"Yes, that should do it," Kat replied cheerfully, her good humor restored by Jordan's obvious annoyance. At least he wasn't ignoring her anymore. "Well, excuse me, will you please? I've got a lot more work to do."

She walked away, biting her lip and trying not to laugh when Leann sent her a surreptitious thumb to forefinger "okay" sign. She ought to feel guilty, she supposed, but she felt just the slightest bit devilish, and more carefree than she had in quite a while.

Maybe that was what she needed, Kat mused as she walked through the crowd taking picture after picture. Maybe if she and Jordan could return to those carefree days when they were first in love, before so much came between them, they could regain what they had lost. But how could she accomplish that when Jordan was obviously determined to keep his distance at all costs? Somehow she had to get close to him, become part of his day-to-day life again.

Kat jerked to a standstill, struck by an idea, an audacious, outrageous idea. Her lips curved upward and she smiled at her own temerity, trying not to laugh out loud. She thought out probabilities and options while she took pictures of the bride and groom toasting each other. She investigated advantages and disadvantages as her camera captured the groom tossing the bride's blue garter to his laughing friends. She mulled over possibilities for success and disaster as she caught the bridal couple making a honeymoon getaway under a shower of rice. And she decided to go for it when the last frame of film was safely stored away in the canister. Just one small detail . . .

She found Bertie in the kitchen overseeing the removal of the buffet as a favor to the bride's exhausted mother. A few minutes of intense conversation in a secluded corner, and Kat strode out of the reception hall with a spring in her step and a smile on her pretty face. If she didn't love Jordan so much, she would almost pity him. After all, the man didn't stand a chance. And on that thought, Kat did laugh out loud.

"You want *what?*"

Kat gave Jordan a look that labeled him only slightly less dense than the marble paperweight she held. Her condescending smile set his teeth on edge.

"I want a job," she said, setting the paperweight back down among the clutter of papers and books on Jordan's desk. On Bertie's advice, she had cornered him the next evening in his home office while he worked on the farm books. "More specifically, I'd like my old job back. I hear you're looking for an experienced hand."

Jordan's heels hit the floor with a thud. "You've got to be joking," he said tightly. "I'm not that desperate!"

"Now, Jordan, don't be too hasty."

"I haven't got time for your little games, Katherine."

Kat frowned. This was going to be harder than she thought. She had to make him see the logic of such an arrangement or he'd never go for it. Maybe she should play on his sympathies, if he had any. She wasn't above a bit of subterfuge to get her way. After all, it was for his own good. Someday he'd thank her for it. She trailed a finger along the edge of his desk and allowed her breath to come out in a shaky sigh while avoiding his eyes.

"Do I have to beg?" she asked in a low voice.

"You really would take a job like this? Why?"

"I like to eat." Her mouth quirked with a hint of self-mockery.

Jordan's eyes narrowed. "I'm not sure I understand. I thought you were determined to open up a studio."

"Oh, I am! But the world isn't exactly beating a path to my door right now. It's going to take some time to get established. And photographic equipment is expensive."

"You mean after all those years of working you have nothing to show for it?"

She shrugged. "Not much. Exciting work, but not so well paid, especially after expenses."

"You should have thought of this before you came home," he pointed out uncomfortably.

"Yes, well . . ." She bit her lip and looked at him, her blue eyes wide and anxious. Jordan rose and walked around the desk.

"Look, if you need money, I'll be glad to lend you—"

"Please, Jordan," Kat said, stiffening, "allow me some pride."

"I don't know what you want me to do," he grumbled.

"Give me the job! You need the help and I'm experienced. Just until the end of breeding season. I'll be on my feet by then."

Or be gone by then, he thought with a pang. He studied her vibrant face for a long moment. "A better solution would be for you to sell me your land."

"No!"

"Katherine, be reasonable. You need the money and I need the pastures."

"No, Jordan. It's the only thing I've got left of Papa John's. I couldn't possibly sell it."

"But your financial worries would be over. You could set up a dozen studios on what I'm willing to pay for it."

Damn! Kat thought. This wasn't going at all as she planned. "Forget it," she said. "I'd sooner go hungry."

"You stubborn wench!" Jordan glowered down at her, jamming his fists into his pockets to keep from touching her. He knew how dangerous that could be.

"No more stubborn than you, counselor! I'm the perfect solution to your problem and you know it. Bertie's told me how much extra work you've had lately. I could help out until you find someone permanently."

"So you and Bertie have been conspiring, have you?"

"You leave Bertie out of this!" Kat railed.

"You brought her up," he pointed out with maddening logic.

"Well, I can see that I'm not getting anywhere with you —you mule-eared lawyer! Thanks for nothing!" She flounced toward the door and missed the sudden twist of his lips.

"Kat, wait." Jordan followed her, his conscience pricked. He couldn't stand the thought of her being in real need.

"What for?" Her chin stuck out at a belligerent angle.

"I take exception to being called mule-eared."

"Count your blessings. That was just a warm-up."

"Look, you know that it just wouldn't work out, don't you?"

"I'm not asking for a lifetime career. Just something to tide me over for a while."

"I appreciate your dilemma, but—"

"There's got to be a way we can compromise," she interrupted, frowning and absently tugging on her earring. Suddenly her expression cleared. "That's it!"

"What's it?" he asked suspiciously.

"Would you take a lease on my pastures? That way I could hold on to the title, couldn't I?"

Jordan smiled in relief. "You'd do that? Great." He named a sum that was the going rate for agricultural leases. "If that's agreeable, I'll draw up the papers tomorrow."

"That sounds fair, and in return you'll give me the job," she said happily.

"Now wait a damn minute! I'll do no such thing."

"Look, you get what you want, I get what I want. Even trade."

"You'll have the lease money. You won't need a job scraping out stalls," he snapped, his irritation rising.

"Uh-uh. Anything I get from your lease goes straight into the studio. There's equipment I need, and I suppose I should look for a van. Not to mention hiring an assistant."

"An assistant? And when do you propose to do all this?"

"Why, after the breeding season, of course. I'll be too busy working at Scott Farms until then."

"Katherine," he said, his voice warning that he was being pushed too far.

"Jordan," she retorted, facing off with him like a boxer. "Take it or leave it, counselor. All or nothing."

"You stubborn—"

"You're repeating yourself, Jordan," she said, holding back a laugh. "That's the first sign of senility, you know."

"Not senility—insanity. You're trying to drive me around the bend with your shenanigans!"

"Oh, be a good sport," she cajoled. "This way we both win."

"You're going to be sorry you started this," he promised, his expression seething with resentment. He was being manipulated, and quite handily, but there was little he could do about it.

"Then it's a deal?" Kat tried to keep the excitement out of her voice.

"Yeah, it's a deal."

"Wonderful! Shake on it." She offered a smile and her hand. "When do I start?"

Jordan accepted her hand, noticing the smoothness of

81

her skin and the way his palm swallowed hers. "Tomorrow morning. Six o'clock."

Kat groaned. "I'd forgotten how early you have to get up."

She tugged her hand and Jordan realized then that he'd been caressing the back of her hand with his thumb. He hastily released her.

"Don't be late. And don't expect any special considerations, either."

"I wouldn't dream of it. I'm not afraid of hard work," she said gaily. She paused beside the door. "Oh, and Jordan?"

"Hmm?"

"Tell Sondra I said hello, will you? Such a cute child."

Jordan felt his ears go red and vowed she'd pay for her little jibe. Proud of herself, was she? Feeling sassy at having gotten around him, too, he'd wager. Well, just wait. He might have a couple of surprises up his sleeve, too. The thought cheered him immensely.

"See you in the morning, Katherine."

Kat blinked, puzzled at his mild reaction, but she didn't have a chance to think about it further because the office door swung open and a slim, chic, silver-haired tornado burst into the room.

"Jordan, I simply must have a moment of your time," Rosalind Scott said crisply. "Don't you ever answer your phone? And I'll be late for my church meeting with Reverend Guilbeau—oh, I'm sorry, dear. I didn't realize you had company."

"I was just on my way out," Kat said, her throat suddenly dry.

"You remember Katherine Holt, don't you, Mother?" Jordan asked.

Rosalind's head snapped in Kat's direction and her eyes widened fractionally. "Why, of course," she murmured with every evidence of pleasure. "How very nice to see you again, my dear."

Kat wasn't fooled for a moment. She'd seen the flicker of nervousness in Rosalind's gray eyes just before they became glacial. She had to hand it to her, though. Rosalind was still the consummate politician's wife, the epitome of Southern graciousness, hiding that steel backbone and cool, incisive mind behind a façade of genteel manners. She was thinking on her feet every minute, although Kat was sure Rosalind was as shocked as she was to come face to face again so unexpectedly after all these years.

What was she thinking? Kat wondered. Did she fear that Kat had come to Jordan with the truth at last? Well, let her sweat. Although certainly Rosalind never did anything so indelicate, Kat thought wryly. Yes, let her wonder, but no matter how much she was tempted to tell Jordan about the bargain Rosalind had struck with her, Kat knew she never would. She couldn't bring herself to inflict that pain all over again. Besides, wasn't it time to go on, to start over? She and Jordan couldn't go back, but they could go forward—together. Wasn't that what her little plan was all about?

Kat gave Rosalind a tight smile, meeting her eyes directly. She saw another flicker of surprise, an instant reassessment. Kat was glad she was not the cowed, intimidated teenager any longer.

"It's always a pleasure, Mrs. Scott," Kat said and shook hands cordially. "If you'll excuse me, I'm sure you want to speak with your son. I'll see you in the morning, Jordan."

"Bright and early," he replied. "I'll see you out."

"Don't bother. I know the way," she said with a smile, then disappeared with a flip of blond hair.

"What did she mean by that?" Rosalind demanded of her tall son.

Jordan went back to his desk and idly picked up a breeding record. "I've hired Katherine to work on the farm."

"Oh, Jordan, no! You can't mean to say you're actually doing that girl a favor, are you? After all she did to you?"

"I don't care to discuss it, Mother." Jordan dropped the paper, then sat down in his swivel chair with a tired sigh.

"I heard she was back, but I can't believe this!"

"It's not what you're thinking."

"Well, what am I to think?" Rosalind demanded.

"Nothing," he said tightly.

Instantly, Rosalind changed her tack. "Oh, Jordan, dear, I don't mean to pry, it's just that I'm worried. It would be a disaster to become involved with that girl again. And I know that I should be charitable, but I find it very hard to forget the pain the Holt family caused your father."

"We can't change the past, and besides, none of that was Katherine's fault," he said. He felt faintly guilty, as if he betrayed his father's memory even as he defended Kat.

"I just don't want to see you hurt again," his mother said earnestly.

"It's nothing like that." Jordan's expression softened at his mother's obvious concern. "She needed a job temporarily and we needed another hand. It's as simple as that."

"Are you sure?" Rosalind was dubious.

"Positive. And in the meantime, she's agreed to lease the Holt place to me. You know we need more room. Katherine plans to open a photography studio eventually. She took some pictures of Don's girls the other day and handled the photography at the McElroy wedding. So you see, this is just a temporary thing."

"I still think it's very foolish," Rosalind said stiffly. Her sulky tone hinted that she was offended Jordan would not listen to her advice.

"Don't worry, it won't last long," Jordan placated her. "Now, tell me what brings you out this evening."

"Well, Reverend Guilbeau . . ."

As Rosalind spoke enthusiastically about her latest community service project Jordan listened halfheartedly. In the back of his mind he planned his strategy for Kat's first day. He'd been sweet-talked and tricked into giving her the damn job, but he hadn't promised to make it pleasant for her. His lips curved upward. Try to manipulate him, would she? Oh, she'd pay—would she ever pay!

CHAPTER SIX

The sun was a peach-colored ball on the horizon when Kat walked over to Scott Farms the next morning. A low-lying haze blanketed the pastures, softening the landscape with a cottony cloud that would burn away quickly as the sun climbed higher. The mares, some with new foals, stamped impatiently at the paddock gates, eager to enter their stalls and receive their morning grain. Kat paused to admire them, tugging her work gloves from the back pocket of her jeans and adjusting the Texas Rangers baseball cap over her ponytail. She drew in a great breath of the sweet morning air and sighed gustily with pleasure.

She followed the muffled sound of men's voices and the clink of tackle into the main barn. Peering into the dim interior, she found Jordan talking quietly with the other hands, his body relaxed, his hands jammed deeply in his jeans pockets.

"Good morning."

He looked up at Kat's soft greeting and gestured her forward. Kat saw the black stubble of beard shadowing his jaw and his dark hair lay rumpled, as if he'd run his hands through it more than once.

"Ready to get started, Katherine?" Jordan asked.

"I'm ready," she replied. "Am I late?"

"A mare foaled just before dawn," Jordan explained succinctly. "Touch and go there for a minute, right, fellows?"

86

The other men muttered their agreement and smiled wearily.

"Are they all right?" she asked.

"Just fine." Jordan tugged her elbow, urging her into the circle as he made introductions. "You remember J.W., don't you?" Kat murmured her agreement and smiled at the grizzled black man. "Pete, Eddie, Jimbo." The younger men nodded shyly as she shook hands. "We're giving you the upper stalls to tend. Ask these fellows if you need anything."

"I remember the routine."

"Good, because everyone's tied up pretty much with foaling. Since we've been short-handed a lot of extra chores have mounted up. I hope you're ready to pitch in."

His white teeth gleamed with a grin that made Kat's eyes narrow. Jordan was up to something, she was sure of it. "That's what I'm here for," she replied.

"Glad to hear it." He clapped her on the back in a companionable manner that did nothing to ease her apprehensions. Then he let her have it, spitting out a list of chores a mile long to do after she finished her regular duties of feeding and cleaning out stalls. "And when you're done with the tack room, you could always sweep the barn kitchen and stack the pop bottles," he concluded.

Kat began to steam. "But—"

"Anything wrong, Katherine?" Jordan asked mildly.

"Nothing." Her teeth came together with a snap. "Not a thing." She'd be damned if she'd give him the satisfaction of complaining. Thought he could drive her away with overwork, did he? Well, he had another think coming!

"Right," he said, grinning. He gave her shoulder a squeeze through the thin cotton of her T-shirt. "I've got to get to the office. Oh, and Katherine? I suggest you trade those sneakers for a pair of rubber boots before you start." Jordan's grin got wider. "You're going to need them."

And she did indeed. Kat was ankle deep in horse dung,

raking out a stall when she saw Jordan pass on his way into town, looking cool and professional in coat and tie. Suddenly she had a sinking feeling that her well-laid plans had gone completely askew.

She was certain of it by the end of the day when Jordan found her in the tack room struggling with a tangle of harnesses and halters, straps and leads. She was salty with sweat, more than a little dirty, and knew she smelled of warm horseflesh. The rubber band on her ponytail had been lost long before and her hair was squashed any which way under her cap.

She cleaned the leather with a rag saturated with saddle soap, muttering imprecations and dire threats against Jordan Scott with each stroke. She jumped when he spoke behind her.

"Talking to yourself, Kat?" Amusement glittered in his eyes.

"Yes!" she snapped, giving him a haughty stare. "Do you mind? It's a private conversation."

Jordan couldn't repress his chuckle. "Really? I'm sure I heard my name mentioned—or was it being taken in vain?"

"You must have been mistaken. It probably has something to do with that overinflated opinion you have of yourself."

Kat definitely felt at a disadvantage. A day in an air-conditioned law office hadn't exactly wilted Jordan. He still looked cool as the proverbial cucumber while she felt as attractive as a baked turnip.

"My, my! What's eating you?" Jordan's lean cheek creased in a mockingly sympathetic grin. "Had a hard day?"

Kat ground her teeth, then managed a sugary smile. "Not at all," she said airily. She hung the buckle of the strap she'd been working on over a nail and reached for the next one. "I'm very busy, so if you'll excuse me . . ."

"Leave it for today. It's getting late."

"Oh, I wouldn't dream of it, Mr. Boss Man, sir!" She rubbed her cloth vigorously over the strap, her words drawling. "Got to finish up in here so I can get on to the sweepin'!"

"I said to leave it," Jordan said, scowling.

"Yes, sir! Anything you say, sir!"

"Katherine, don't push me!" Jordan's hand shot out and he hauled her out of the tack room.

"Just aimin' to please, Boss Man," Kat retorted.

"You can please me by holding that damned viperish tongue of yours!" Jordan roared.

What was it about this woman that sent him over the edge in just a matter of seconds? he wondered. Being near Kat shot his control all to hell, reducing him to a blithering idiot. His reputation as the coolest courtroom attorney in ten parishes would be smashed to bloody smithereens if his associates could see him now. He released her arm, disgusted at himself.

"Whatever you say, Bo—whatever you say," Kat amended hastily. She glanced away from the thunderous tilt of Jordan's thick brows. "Was there something you wanted?"

Jordan pinched the bridge of his nose tiredly and tried to remember why he'd come to find her. "Oh, yeah. What did the vet say about Lady Sabrina?"

"No change. She could foal any time or take another week or two." Kat fell into step beside Jordan, glancing uneasily at him. She was sorry she'd antagonized him, seeing how fatigued he was. After all, he'd helped with a foaling in the predawn hours.

"Keep a close watch on her, will you, Katherine? I'm not sure how she'll do now that she's totally blind."

"I will. Thank you for trusting me with her," she added quietly.

The corner of Jordan's mouth twisted upward. "You

were always kindred souls. I think you'll pick up on any changes before anyone else would."

"What if she goes into labor during the night?"

"I've got a man who acts as night watchman during foaling season. He keeps tabs and alerts me or J.W. if one of the mares is in trouble."

"I'd forgotten how hectic it can get," Kat murmured.

"Yeah, nobody gets much sleep, that's for sure," he agreed wryly.

"That can't do your law practice much good."

"It hasn't been too bad, but I'm to the point where I need to hire a full-time manager for the farm or close up shop during the breeding season. My clients probably wouldn't appreciate that, though."

"Then why don't you hire that manager?"

Jordan shrugged and grimaced sheepishly, looking so boyish that Kat's heart twisted. "I don't know, except that it's hard to let go of the reins, so to speak. Besides, it's the most exciting season of the year. Birth, new life—I'd hate to miss it. You know what I mean?"

Kat nodded, her eyes glowing softly. "I know."

Jordan saw the empathy in her expression and knew that she did. There had never been anyone who understood him the way Kat had. But that was a long time ago, he reminded himself sharply. He tore his gaze away from hers. "Why don't you go on home now?"

"I think I will," Kat said. She pulled off her cap and let her hair fall free. She rubbed a rueful hand through it and wrinkled her nose. "I could use a bath."

Jordan looked at her, then sniffed exaggeratedly, a devilish glint in his toffee-colored eyes. "So I noticed."

Kat felt her indignation rise. "Well! Put in an honest day's work outdoors instead of sitting behind a desk and we'll see how sweet *you* smell, counselor! Excuse me!" She swept past him, regal as any queen, her nose in the air.

Jordan watched her march off with a twinkle of reluctant

admiration in his eye. Indomitable, invincible Kat. "See you in the morning," he called.

The worst thing about working on a horse farm, Kat decided, was that she never got a day off. A horse didn't care if it was Saturday or Sunday. Weekends meant nothing to an animal whose sole concern was filling its stomach twice a day. One week melted into two weeks, and still Sabrina hadn't foaled, although there had been a rash of births and many nights when none of the crew, including Kat, had gotten any sleep. Kat knew it was a form of natural protection for mares to foal at night, but it took a toll on their human caretakers. Still, it was an exhilarating time.

Kat had the routine down pat, and she knew all the mares in her care now. They were becoming accustomed to her and gave her little trouble, allowing her to check them and their offspring thoroughly and even attend to the worming and doses of vitamins. She fed them twice a day, then turned them out to pasture on the lush grass. Keeping busy between feeding times was no problem, and she pitched in wherever she was needed. Although she was still picking up a lot of slack when the men were busy with a new foal or breeding a mare to Jordan's stallion, Jordan had stopped looking for extra chores for her to do. In fact, she had even caught him looking at her with approval more than once.

That was encouraging, she decided, even though they had been too busy to do more than bicker in passing. Her heart continued to thump out of control whenever he was around, and although her emotions were never far from the surface, she tried to suppress them with hard work. She kept telling herself that this was exactly what she needed, a sort of hiatus, a chance for her and Jordan to grow accustomed to each other's presence without the emotional pressures of one-on-one encounters.

Perversely, she began to grow annoyed with Jordan's

standoffish attitude and wondered how to catch his attention. She was hard pressed to look glamorous at six o'clock every morning, and it was even worse by the end of a hot, busy day. She wondered sometimes if she was doing her cause more harm than good by working at Scott Farms, little realizing that she had lost that white, pinched look and now glowed with good health and a sun-kissed radiance. Misgivings about the wisdom of her plan plagued her. Still, how else was she going to get close and stay close to Jordan? At least while she worked for him he couldn't ignore her completely.

Kat also reaped the benefits of being close to Bertie. The older woman was a self-appointed committee of one to provide support and sustenance to Katherine Holt. Most days, Bertie would come wandering down the drive with a lunch pail for Kat and they often shared it in the barn, sitting on the old painted ladderback chairs and feeding tidbits to the barn cats. Occasionally during the day, Bertie would follow Kat around the stalls, gossiping and catching her up on all the Mansfield news, and Kat appreciated those visits most of all. Working out at the farm was a very insular existence, and other than the hands, Bertie, and a few phone conversations with Leann, Kat had very little contact with the outside world.

"You're going to have to get out more in the evenings," Bertie admonished one afternoon. "You didn't come all the way back home to become a hermit."

"Oh, Bertie! I can barely drag myself home and into a cool tub most days," Kat protested.

"See there? I knew your sweet-talking Jordan into this job wasn't a good idea! And now you've signed that there lease and got a tidy sum in the bank to boot. There's no reason for you to slave away out here. But you know me, I never say anything!"

"Really, I am enjoying it," Kat said, and somewhat to her own surprise she found that it was true. "This is what I needed—to get back to basics. The simple truths, the animals, some dirt under my fingernails. I can't quite explain," Kat said, breaking off with a laugh.

"Well, if you wanted dirt, you certainly came to the right place," Bertie quipped, folding the piece of aluminum foil around the brownies she'd brought. "Have you been painting at night again?"

"Why?" Kat laughed. "Have I got a smudge on my face?"

"Nope. Elbow."

Kat laughed and struggled to see the black paint on the tip of her elbow. "Oh, Lord, I thought I'd gotten it all off."

"Look here, girl," Bertie fussed, "you can't work day and half the night and then go home and try to work there, too."

"I've got to get that darkroom painted somehow," Kat replied. "How else will I ever get the business going?" She popped a final bite of brownie into her mouth and stood, stretching luxuriously. It was the midafternoon lull. J.W. had gone home, and the others were lazing around somewhere snoozing on the hay bales.

"If I was you I'd worry less about that and more about how I was going to get Jordan to pay some attention to me," Bertie snorted. "Did you know that Sondra woman was over yesterday evening again? Just barges right in, bold as brass."

"You really shouldn't tell me this," Kat protested faintly, a bolt of pure jealousy surging through her.

"Of course, Jordan's too much of a gentleman to throw her out," Bertie continued blithely, "so she chatters away like a jay bird and ends up staying for supper. I just don't know what that man sees in her!"

"She is very pretty," Kat pointed out.

"Entirely too prissy for my taste. Always worried about chipping her nail polish." The older woman sniffed disdainfully.

"Yes, but it's Jordan's taste that counts," Kat sighed, suddenly despondent. How could she hope to win Jordan's affections stuck down at the barn while doe-eyed Sondra had the run of the house?

"Well, with his mother pushing them together at every opportunity, *someone* had better try diverting his interest," Bertie said significantly.

"I'm not going to throw myself at Jordan!" Kat hesitated at Bertie's skeptical look. "Well, not exactly. I thought working closely with him might—I don't know, help somehow. But for all the notice I've gotten lately I might as well be one of the boys."

"You could start by washing off some of that dirt," Bertie said tartly. She hauled herself off her chair, then paused to wipe her gold-wire glasses on her gingham apron. She tugged the wire frames over her ears and eyed Kat's plaid shirt and jeans critically. "And wear something a little more—you know, feminine."

Kat laughed out loud. "To the barn? No, Aunt Bertie, I'm not going to try to compete with Sondra. That's not my style. And one Sondra is certainly enough!"

"You're right about that!" Bertie chuckled and her hazel eyes sparkled. "Well, I'll leave you to your devilment. I just hope you know what you're doing, but you know I never say anything."

Kat laughed and waved as Bertie walked back to the main house. She did have a point, Kat thought, rubbing a knuckle thoughtfully over one grimy cheek. It certainly wouldn't hurt to tidy up a bit. Not that she was doing it for anyone but herself. No, sir! Let Jordan Scott find his pleasure with that redheaded floozy. See if Kat Holt cared!

Kat marched down the line of enclosed wooden stalls, slamming the doors to the empty stalls one after the other to punctuate her thoughts. Outside she turned on a hose, then bent over the deep galvanized water trough and splashed her heated cheeks.

"Well, well," Jordan's deep voice drawled. "May a gentleman enter milady's boudoir?"

Kat jerked upright, water dripping from her face, down her neck, and into the light cotton of her shirt. Her irritation rose in direct proportion to the height of Jordan's mockingly raised eyebrow. Why did he always have to catch her at a disadvantage?

"That depends," she snapped. She gave an exaggerated look around. "Where's the gentleman?"

"You're awfully thin-skinned lately, Katherine. What's the matter? Finding the work here more than you bargained for?" He grinned and folded his arms, stretching the white fabric of his dress shirt across his muscular shoulders. It was clear he had come from the office although he had discarded his tie and jacket. His long legs were braced aggressively and he seemed to exude confidence. Kat swallowed against the tug of his attraction, instinctively countering her response to him with the sharp edge of her tongue.

"I'm just surprised that you decided to grace us with your presence, counselor." Her expression was faintly mocking as she smoothed her hair, tucking the wayward tresses behind her ears. Jordan's eyes narrowed and his gaze dropped to the upthrust tilt of her breasts accentuated by her damp shirt. Kat hurriedly dropped her arms, flushing at the knowing glint in Jordan's eyes. She plucked self-consciously at the front of her shirt, annoyed that her flesh tingled at his merest glance. This certainly wasn't going according to plan!

"I've been known to put in an hour or two now and then," he said dryly. He nodded toward the water trough and his smile became slightly malicious. "I'm pleased to see that your personal habits are improving."

"Oh!" she exclaimed, outraged as his jibe struck home. She stomped around the trough and grabbed the hose with the intention of turning it off. "I've got more important

95

things to worry about than chipping my nail polish! I find it disgusting the way some men drool over every over-made-up Lolita that comes along!"

"Lolita!" Jordan laughed. "Why, Katherine! If I didn't know better I'd say you were jealous."

"Me? Ha!" Kat gave an incredulous laugh. "Don't flatter yourself."

"Whatever you say, honey." His smug expression infuriated her even further. His gaze raked her and his smile was slow, sensual. When he spoke, the husky timbre of his voice raised the tiny hairs on the back of her neck. "Anyway, you should remember my technique is fastidious. I never drool. I savor every delicious morsel."

Kat gasped. "You, sir, are an oversexed goat! You might try cold showers as a remedy! In fact . . ." She glanced at the hose in her hand.

"Don't even think it, Kat," Jordan warned.

Kat didn't hesitate. Raising the nozzle, she sprayed him with all her might. She whooped at Jordan's stunned countenance. He should have known she'd never shirk a direct challenge!

"Damnation, woman!" Jordan thundered.

"It's just what the doctor ordered, Jordan. Painless and economical!"

Thoroughly soaked, he leaped through the deluge, struggling with her for control of the spraying hose. They grappled for the nozzle, Kat shrieking with laughter until they were both drenched.

Finally, by dint of superior strength and intent, Jordan wrested the offending hose from his tormentor, holding a half-drowned Kat by the scruff of her shirt. Water dripped off his aristocratic nose and his shirt front was soaked, as were his slacks and expensive loafers. He was furious.

"You and your juvenile sense of humor," he grumbled ominously.

Unrepentant, Kat pushed a soaking strand of blond hair

from her eyes and squirmed in his grasp. Her grin was impish. "You deserved it."

"If you insist on acting like a child, then you'll just have to take your punishment like one," Jordan growled. He turned off the hose, and without releasing her shirt collar, grabbed the waistband of her jeans and hauled her unceremoniously toward the stalls.

"Wait, Jordan," Kat half laughed, half pleaded. "What are you going to do?"

"Send you to your room." He gave her a hoist through a stall door, sending her sprawling headfirst into the pile of straw on the floor.

Kat landed with a thump and scrambled up immediately, but it was too late. Jordan slammed the wooden stall door and slipped the latch, locking her in.

"Jordan Scott! You open this door!" Kat demanded, beating on the door with both fists. She could see the top of his head over the tall wooden planks that formed the walls separating the stalls. Overhead the rafters of the barn rose to meet the tin roof.

"Not until you've learned a lesson. Try to drown me, will you? Good grief, I must have a quart of water in each shoe!"

Kat tried cajoling him through the cracks in the stall door, but she couldn't keep the amusement from her voice. "I didn't mean it, Jordan. Let me out? I promise to be good."

"Naughty little girls must take their medicine," he returned.

"Jordan," she laughed. "Let me out!"

"When you've had time to reflect on your transgressions."

"I've got things to do," she wheedled.

"So do I. Be seeing you." The top of his head disappeared.

"Jordan! Damn you!"

97

She kicked the door in frustration, then grabbed her bruised toes with both hands and hopped around the stall. Releasing her throbbing foot, she limped to the opposite wall and leaned against the protruding feed bin. She felt the way she had as a kid when Jordan was trouncing her at marathon Monopoly: Go Directly to Jail. Do Not Pass Go. Do Not Collect $200.

Well, she'd show him!

Kat climbed into the feed bin and grasped the top edge of the wall. Agilely, she levered herself up. Clinging to a rafter for support, she began to walk tightrope style across the supporting beams.

"What the hell do you think you're doing?"

Kat suppressed a start of surprise at Jordan's yell and continued to set one foot ahead of the other on the narrow rafter. She cast a baleful glare down into his anxious face. "Don't you know it's dangerous to break someone's concentration?" she snapped.

"Get down from there before you break your fool neck!"

She presented Jordan with an exceedingly childish and totally satisfying expression of her disdain. She stuck her tongue out at him. "Make me."

"You stubborn—"

"When did you become such an old fuddy-duddy?" Kat asked, continuing her stroll, arms outstretched for balance. "We used to do this all the time."

"That was before we knew any better. Kids bounce, but adults break, or hadn't you heard?" His voice was laced with sarcasm. He began to peel off his soaked shirt.

"Jordan is a 'fraidy cat," she singsonged.

"You're not too big to spank, you know."

"Try it, buster!"

"That does it!" He threw his shirt down and vaulted up, catching a rafter and pulling himself up after her.

Kat gave a small shriek and walked faster. She could tell from the steely glint in Jordan's eyes that there would be hell to pay for this bit of mischief. It would be best if she disappeared entirely—and at once.

"Don't think you're going to get away with this," he muttered from behind her.

"I didn't—" Kat's words broke off with a high scream as she reached for footing and found only air.

Jordan saw her fall, disappearing into the stall below. There was a thump and rustle, then silence. Fear clogged his heart. "Oh, damn!"

He jumped down from the beam and raced around to the stall, his heart in his throat. Had that damned stubborn woman really broken her neck this time?

She lay facedown in the pile of golden straw. Jordan knelt beside her, his hands shaking. Grasping her shoulders, he gently rolled her over. Her eyes were closed.

"Kat! Can you hear me?" he rasped. "For God's sake, are you all right?"

Kat's eyelashes flickered and a slow grin stretched across her lips. "Never better." She laughed softly and her blue eyes opened finally, glittering up at him with suppressed amusement.

"You dirty, lowdown . . . You did that on purpose," he accused, tightening his grip on her shoulders. "You scared me out of a year's growth!"

"You can spare it," she pointed out, giggling.

"There's nothing funny about this! You could have been seriously hurt." Jordan's eyes darkened ominously. "You need to be taught a lesson, young lady! I said you weren't too old to spank."

"Don't you dare!" Kat gasped, suddenly aware of her precarious position. She attempted to roll away, but Jordan held her firmly.

"It would be no more than you deserve," he observed. He gave a sudden, wicked grin. "But I know a more suitable punishment."

"Now wait a min—Jordan!" she yelped. "What are you

doing? Stop that! You know I can't stand to be . . . tickled!"

Jordan's fingers traveled over her rib cage, tickling her unmercifully through her damp shirt. Kat shrieked with laughter and doubled up, trying to evade the relentless onslaught.

"Try to drown me, will you?" Jordan laughed.

"I didn't mean it, I swear!" Kat gasped and tried to pry his fingers loose. "Oh! You mean, hateful—"

"Careful, Kat! Or you'll just get more of the same!"

"Despicable bully! Oh!" Heaving with laughter, Kat rolled to her knees, twisting and arching to escape his torture. She pushed at him and her hands met the damp skin of his bare chest. It was time to fight fire with fire, she decided, working her fingers into the taut flesh of his stomach.

"Hey!" Jordan whooped in surprise.

"See how you like some of your own medicine!" Kat declared, turning to the attack, her fingers seeking those sensitive spots on his abdomen, under his arms, at the back of his knees. They rolled and tussled playfully, each trying to gain the advantage, all the while laughing so hard the breath rasped from their chests.

Finally, with one huge lunge, Jordan pinned Kat flat on her back, his hands holding her wrists over her head, his legs over hers and the weight of his body holding her down effortlessly.

"Say uncle," he gasped.

"Never!"

"Say calf rope."

"No!" Kat's giggles slowed and her breathlessness was suddenly not just because of her recent exertion.

"Say let me up, Jordan, pretty please," he demanded with a wide grin. His face was inches from hers and he knew he'd won the contest physically, yet he continued to enjoy the battle of wills.

"Uh-uh." She shook her head.

"Then we'll stay here until you do."

"Is that a promise?" she murmured.

Kat met his eyes and saw the sudden golden flare behind his caramel-colored gaze. Awareness sizzled down every nerve fiber. All laughter faded away, replaced by the intimate knowledge of his hard chest crushing her soft breasts, his long leg insinuated between hers, his warm breath on her face. Kat's eyes dropped without volition to Jordan's lips. With an inarticulate groan, Jordan lowered his mouth to hers.

The kiss was sweet, infinitely tender, evoking a response in Kat that she could not and did not try to deny. In the blackness behind her closed eyelids, silver stars whisked away in a shower of spangles and she felt weightless, floating free in space and sensation, anchored only by the solid mass that was Jordan.

She shuddered slightly at the soft yet insistent probe of his tongue, then yielded, giving herself up to the comet's flare and rush of urgency that centered itself low in her womb. She reached for him, but Jordan's hands still held her wrists immobile, and then she was unable to do anything but *feel*.

The sweep of his tongue inside her sensitive mouth made her moan into his mouth. He released her wrists and his hands explored the carved arc of her waist, her rounded breasts beneath the damp fabric of her blouse. His fingers brushed the tender peaked nubs and Kat arched against his hands, desire and need rocketing through her with the speed of light.

Jordan lifted his head slowly and Kat opened weighted lids, gazing up at him with dazed blue eyes. Her hands lay beside her head, free now, fingers curled into her palms, vulnerable and childlike. Jordan's breathing was harsh, matching the erratic rise and fall of her chest.

She looked at him, her gaze hesitant, almost quizzical,

her mouth soft and defenseless. Her eyes asked a question for which Jordan as yet had no answer. The lines of his face were taut with need, a need that found an answering chord in Kat.

"Who started this, anyway?" he murmured, his voice husky. He reached up and began to pick bits of straw out of her hair, piece by piece.

"I—I don't remember," she whispered.

His fingers faltered on her hair, stroking the silky locks, then he dipped his head once more. A hairsbreadth away from her lips, he paused. "Then we'll both finish it."

Kat's silent sigh of agreement was smothered by an agitated shout from outside the barn.

"Good God Almighty! Boss, come quick!"

Jordan muttered a curse and reluctantly rolled off Kat. He pulled her to her shaky feet, his gaze apologetic. Kat turned her back to him, feeling the shaming color stain her cheeks, and brushed the straw from her sodden jeans and tangled hair. She didn't know whether to laugh or cry at this sudden reprieve. Would she really have let Jordan make love to her there on the hay, without a word of love spoken between them? She honestly didn't know, but the possibility frightened her nearly as much as the threat of living without him.

Jordan stepped out of the stall. "Yeah, Pete, what is it?"

The young man hurried forward. "Ain't never seen anything like it, Boss! Looks like Lady Sabrina's gonna foal right out there in broad daylight!"

Kat's head snapped around. Sabrina? Now? Oh, no!

"All right, Pete. We're coming." Jordan was suddenly all business. He cast a grim glance toward Kat. "Come on, Kat. We're going to need your help."

CHAPTER SEVEN

"Dammit! Will you hold her, Kat!" Jordan snapped.

"I'm trying!"

Sabrina lay on her side, her sides heaving, her flanks wet with placental water. Kat struggled to quiet the straining mare, holding her head while Jordan and J.W. worked at the other end. Kat's fingers clenched on the leather halter and beads of sweat rolled down her brow. Things were happening fast—too fast.

Sabrina had picked the far corner of her paddock to have her baby, but as usual the mares in the adjoining paddocks knew something was going on. Several hung their heads over the fence to form an equine audience. The excitement had brought forth the other hands to watch as well, and neither group was helping Sabrina's state of mind. The mare nickered urgently and rolled her blind eyes.

"She thinks the other horses are too close," Kat panted. "I wish there were some way she could understand she's safe."

"Just try to keep her quiet," Jordan said. He made a sound of satisfaction. "It won't be long now. Here's the bubble."

Kat twisted around, trying to see the leading edge of the placental sack.

"There's a foot, Boss," J.W. said.

Suddenly, Jordan swore. "Damn!"

"What is it?" Kat demanded.

"Only one foot. Damn! The other must be turned back under."

"Can you turn it?" Kat asked anxiously.

"Got to try," Jordan said. On his knees, he went to work, gently pushing his hand into the body of the uterus, searching for the other foot, fighting the strong muscular contractions. He grimaced with the exertion. "There! Got it!" He moved back, satisfied with the twin hoofs now appearing, pushed farther and farther out by each contraction.

"There's the nose!" J.W. said excitely. He and Jordan began to peel the remains of the placental sack away from the foal's nose.

"Look at her push. That's right, girl, push all the fluid out of his lungs!" Jordan encouraged.

"Here it comes!" J.W. shouted.

With a final heave, the mare expelled her burden, a wet, glistening bundle of dark hide and bones. The new foal quivered, struggled, then took its first breath. For a few moments everyone, horse and human alike, rested. The mare lifted her head and nickered.

"Easy girl. Your baby's okay." Kat stroked Sabrina's neck, knowing it would be bad for the foal if its mother got up too soon, interrupting the supply of blood flowing into the baby through the umbilical cord.

Jordan grunted in satisfaction. "There, he broke the cord. Get that clamp on it, J.W., and I'll burn the end with iodine. You can let her go now, Kat," Jordan said. Kat released the halter and moved back. Almost immediately the mare made an attempt to get to her feet. In five minutes she was standing, then she began to lick her new baby from ear to hoof.

They smiled together, standing beside the fence, basking in a job well done.

"A colt." Jordan's voice held an element of pride.

"He's beautiful, isn't he?" Kat breathed. "Oh, look! He's trying to get to his feet already!" The colt reeled drunkenly on his tiny hoofs, then promptly fell over.

"Oowee!" J.W. laughed. "That there's one fine runnin' boy, I guarantee."

"I think you're right, J.W.," Jordan agreed, clapping the older man on the back in mutual congratulation. "Just look at how straight his legs are."

The men discussed the various fine merits of the colt, the depth of his chest, the intelligence in his eyes, the width of his nostrils, while Kat listened with only half an ear. It occurred to her that the colt's roan coat, brown mixed with red, was nearly the color of Jordan's hair. *A rust-colored colt for Rusty*, she mused. It was almost like sharing the birth of a child. Would a son of Jordan's have that bewitching tint of red, too? Or could a daughter hope to inherit her mother's honey-gold mop? Alarmed at the direction her thoughts had taken her, Kat shook her head to send that fancy spinning back where it belonged.

They tended to the other birthing routine chores of cleaning up and giving the injections. They all gave a sigh of relief when the colt finally got to his feet and began to take wobbly steps around the pen. A tiny frown formed between Kat's brows and she squinted against the glare of the early-afternoon sun. The baby obviously wanted to nurse, but without Sabrina's instinctive guidance he was having difficulty locating the nipple. Kat relaxed when Sabrina turned, sniffed her baby, and nickered gently. Thus encouraged, the little one found what he wanted and was soon sucking eagerly.

"Something wrong?" Jordan asked at her side.

"Well, I don't know." She shrugged. "I'm a little worried, I guess. Will Sabrina be able to take care of him?"

"That remains to be seen, but I don't know why not."

"But she's blind, Jordan. Why, anything could happen!"

"Blind or not, she's got a mother's instincts."

"Yes, but we can't keep them penned indefinitely, and then what if he wanders off? How would she find him?"

"Don't borrow trouble. Nothing's going to happen," Jordan assured her. His casual dismissal of her concerns infuriated her.

"I don't think you really care," she accused. "Just as long as you get another racehorse, nothing else matters!"

"Don't be ridiculous. Of course I care. These are valuable animals," Jordan began, a bit bewildered at her attack.

"That's just it! To you they're just animals, nothing more. You don't think they have feelings and fears, too." Kat felt a sting of tears behind her eyes. "Oh, forget it! You don't understand!"

She stamped off in a huff. Jordan caught J.W.'s eye and shrugged. Their unspoken consensus was one word: Women!

Kat took out her frustration with Jordan by attacking her delayed afternoon chores with a vengeance. When she at last hung up her rake and surveyed the line of clean stalls, the sun was a hot ball hanging just over the trees. She was bone tired after such an eventful day, but she decided to check on Sabrina and the colt one last time before leaving for home.

Kat took a moment to wash her hands and wipe her face at the water trough, straightening her stained and wrinkled apparel as well as she could. A tiger-striped barn cat lay curled in a feed box, busily washing her face. A cluster of Banty chickens scratched in the dirt outside the stalls and clucked desultorily before wandering off to roost for the night. Kat went into the small area that served as a tack room for her stalls and carefully marked down the day's information on the charts thumbtacked to the board walls. Aching in every joint, she stretched, wincing as her tired muscles protested. A couple of hay bales stacked beside the wall beckoned her invitingly.

Just for a minute, she promised herself, stretching out on the prickly bales with a groan. She gave a tired sigh. So much had happened today! It seemed nearly impossible to believe Jordan had kissed her with such tenderness and passion just a few short hours before. Surely he had been motivated by more than plain desire? There had been some kinder feelings involved, she was positive, not just an urge for revenge. A shiver thrilled down her spine at the memory. Maybe, just maybe, he was beginning to forgive her, to trust her and his feelings again. She allowed herself a tiny smile of hope, then snuggled her cheek against her arm and imagined what it would be like loving Jordan and being loved in return. If only Jordan weren't so analytical and logical. No matter how close he came, she always had the feeling that he was keeping part of himself in reserve. If only he could let go of his emotions . . .

Finding Kat asleep a short while later, Jordan wondered how it was possible for a grown woman to look so helpless and appealing and so damned sexy at the same time. He stood over her sleeping form, letting his eyes roam uninhibitedly over her slim but totally feminine shape. With her arm curled under her head she looked like a child, but Jordan knew how much of a woman she could be.

Damn! Why had he let things get so out of control earlier? Hadn't he vowed to let her alone? He'd managed to keep a healthy distance between them until today. It was like an atomic reaction when that distance diminished. Her merest touch was enough to make him burst into flames. He ought to know better than to let that happen. His mouth hardened with resolve. He had to put that distance back for his sanity's sake.

His palm landed with a resounding smack on Kat's denim-clad bottom.

"Ow! What the—" Kat started and slid off the hay bale,

107

landing hard on the dirt floor. She glared angrily up at Jordan. "Why'd you do that?"

"Sleeping on the job. Strictly forbidden."

"You have got some nerve!" she fumed, gathering herself up and dusting herself off as best she could. "You're just mad because you got a soaking!"

"I wouldn't hold a grudge over a little thing like that."

"Oh, no?" Kat's tone was clearly skeptical. She rubbed her stinging behind.

"No, I prefer larger issues."

Kat's expression was suddenly stricken and she turned away, unable to break the unexpectedly awkward silence. Jordan cleared his throat and his next words strove for lightness. "Best be warned, Bertie's steamed about the mess you made of my clothes."

"Are they ruined?" Kat asked in a small voice. Her anxious glance flicked over him, noting absently that he was just as appealing in jeans and a cotton shirt as in more formal attire. "I'm sorry."

"It's nothing the cleaners can't fix." He caught the tip of her chin in his strong fingers and lifted her face, then grinned crookedly. "Besides, it was a small price to pay for our little romp."

Stung, Kat slapped his hand away. Was that all it had been to him? A romp? "Glad you enjoyed it," she said tightly. "I do my best to keep the Boss Man happy."

"Your best?" Jordan laughed softly. "You forget, Katherine, I've seen you do much, much better."

Kat's strangled cry was one of inarticulate outrage and underlying hurt. She brushed past him, too angry and wounded to care if he saw how deep his taunts cut. "Get out of my way. I'm going home."

He caught her elbow, stopping her easily and swinging her around. "But you haven't finished your chores," he admonished in a mocking tone.

"For your information, I'm through for the day, Boss

Man." She jerked her arm free, glowering at him, azure eyes bright with indignation.

"There's still one job left to do."

She looked at him suspiciously. "What?"

"This." He dangled a leather strap with a bucket on it in front of her. A silver sleigh bell jutted from the strap's center, although what a sleigh bell was doing in the steamy depths of Louisiana was beyond Kat.

"What in the world is that for?" she murmured, taking the strap from him. The bell jingled merrily and Kat turned a puzzled gaze to Jordan.

"You've heard of belling the cat, haven't you?" She nodded. "Well, we're going to bell the baby. Sabrina's baby."

"It's a collar!" In her excitement and growing comprehension, her annoyance with Jordan was almost forgotten. "Do you think it will work?"

"Only one way to find out."

Elongated, day's end shadows followed them to Sabrina's paddock. The western horizon glowed with a ruddy light, catching the red highlights in Jordan's dark hair and setting them on fire. Kat found herself clutching the leather collar tightly to keep from reaching out and smoothing back the rich thickness of his hair. If only things could be that simple and free once more. Why did Jordan have to ruin things all over again just when she thought they were getting better?

"Will you do it?" Jordan asked.

Kat nodded and climbed through the fence, speaking softly to Sabrina. The mare's ears pricked up at her familiar voice. The new colt rested on the hay nearby. He raised his head at Kat's approach, then struggled to his wobbly legs. Using her voice and the soothing stroke of her hands, Kat quieted the quivering baby, then gently slipped the collar around his neck and secured the buckle. Moving slowly so as not to startle the nervous pair, Kat retreated, climbing through the fence to rejoin Jordan.

"You definitely have a way about you, Katherine," Jordan said, shaking his head slightly in admiration.

"I love the animals," she said simply. "Oh, look."

The mare snuffled about her baby, then he wobbled forward, interested and curious about the strange two-legged creatures on the other side of his fence. The little bell trilled with every step he took, and Kat nearly laughed at his almost human puzzlement at the new sound. Sabrina's ears perked forward and she nickered nervously for her baby, then trotted unerringly toward the colt.

"It's going to work!" Kat breathed, biting her lip to hold back her jubilation. Sabrina nosed the colt, guiding the hungry baby to nurse as naturally as a sighted mare. Kat could hardly contain herself. "Oh, Jordan!" she bubbled, bouncing up and down in her delight. "It's going to work!" She caught his shoulders and did a little jig.

"Whoa, Kat!" He laughed, steadying her, his hands on her waist.

Her laughter mingled with his. "Your wonderful idea is going to work!" Impulsively, she reached up on tiptoe and kissed him soundly. Her face held a soft inner radiance when she pulled back, for she had discovered something. "You do care," she murmured.

His expression reflected an uncertainty, a slightly abashed quality at odds with the masculine strength of his face. Kat hugged him, pressing her cheek into the cotton of his shirt, smelling the musky tang of honest sweat and the unique scent of his skin.

"Oh, Rusty, you do care," she repeated on a tremulous note.

"Is that so surprising?" His voice was gruff.

She pulled away, shaking her head. Her smile quirked upward. "Not to me, you old fraud."

"Kat . . ."

"Don't try to make excuses," she laughed. "I may not

110

quite understand you, but then I'm not certain you understand yourself."

"You're seeing things that just aren't there," he warned.

"You forget that I'm trained to see things others don't." Her voice was soft, but her eyes were alight with humor. "It's been quite a day, hasn't it? I think I'll go home. 'Bye, Jordan." She waved, winked, and then sauntered off, her steps light and almost jaunty.

Jordan watched her go with mounting frustration, half afraid he'd lost a battle he'd been fighting, not against her, but himself.

"You're spoiling him."

Kat stopped scratching the colt's muzzle, whirled and hid her hands like a guilty child. "I am not."

"Just like you used to do with Sabrina," Jordan said.

"Well . . . maybe." Her smile was a bit sheepish.

In the days since the colt's birth, Kat had spent every spare minute at Sabrina's paddock. Somehow, she became more and more fascinated each day with Sabrina's offspring. Mother and colt had adjusted to Jordan's bell with such ease that it was amazing. The frisky colt often led his mother around the paddock almost like a seeing-eye dog. The only problem was that they were still separated from the herd of mares and foals. The colt saw the other foals romping and galloping in the next paddock and wanted to join in the games. He had become adept at letting his frustrations be known with loud whinnying, and would rush up to meet Kat whenever she appeared to receive her attention and sympathy.

"I can't say that I blame you," Jordan said. "There's something special about this one." He reached through the fence to pat the foal.

Kat gave him a sideways glance, taking in the neat tennis shorts and striped knit shirt he wore on this sultry, sunny Saturday afternoon. Her lids fanned down for an instant and her mouth was suddenly a little dry. Why did he have to be so damned attractive? His strongly muscled legs were darkly bronzed and lightly covered with soft hair that matched that on his forearms. Kat gritted her teeth. Jordan had been so assiduously proper after their last flaming encounter. He never came near her if she was alone, was always polite and distant in company. She was faintly surprised that he was here now, though she had been merely killing time at Sabrina's paddock before going home for the day. Maybe the quiet Saturday had driven him out of his solitary study from whatever lonely endeavor he pursued. But the thought that he had sought her out strictly from boredom was enough to drive a woman mad—or make her fling her love-starved body at him! Kat suppressed an inner smile. No, she wouldn't do that. It was enough that things were easier between them. No more flaming rows. She was prepared to be patient—but not forever.

"He's smart, too." Kat continued the innocuous topic of Sabrina's superior offspring. At least it was a safe, neutral topic.

"Smart, and fast, too. He'll make a grand racer."

"Grand." Kat kept her eyes fastened on the colt. Since when had it felt so awkward to talk? All her words had dried up like a mud puddle in the Sahara. "So, what have you been doing today?" She nearly groaned at the inanity of her question.

"Research for a trial. Some book work. Birth registrations."

"Ah, have you thought of a name for him yet?" Kat reached down to pluck a stem of Johnsongrass and used it to gesture toward the colt.

"As a matter of fact, no." Jordan lounged against the fence, focusing on her fingers nervously stripping leaves off the grass stem. "Would you like to name him?"

Kat's eyes widened and her lips parted. "Oh, could I?"

Jordan chuckled softly at the sudden light of anticipation in her face. "Sure. Any inspirations?"

"I don't know," Kat said, frowning thoughtfully. "What's his sire's name?"

"Calcutta Red."

"Hmm."

"If you're going to take this so seriously, maybe you'd like to look at his breeding records," Jordan suggested with an indulgent chuckle.

"It's quite a responsibility. I want to do it right."

"Well, come on up to the house and you can look them over." Jordan stood away from the fence, jamming his hands down into the deep pockets of his shorts.

"Now?" Kat's glance was hesitant. Was this the chance she had been hoping for when she asked for a job at the farm?

"Sure, why not?"

Why not indeed? Kat thought. Maybe she could somehow push past Jordan's determination to keep their relationship impersonal and reestablish the old friendship, the basis for everything that had grown out of it. She smiled.

"All right."

Kat stepped away from the fence, then looked up at the sound of a car barreling up Jordan's driveway, horn blaring. A low-slung red convertible overflowing with people appeared through a cloud of trailing dust. The car careened past the paddock area, shrill laughter floating across the distance to grate on Kat's ears. The convertible braked sharply, bringing forth a series of shrieks, then reversed until it was even with where she and Jordan stood. With a sinking sensation, Kat noticed that Sondra sat at the wheel, vivacious and effervescent behind white sunglasses and chartreuse hair bow.

"There you are!" Sondra squealed, her peach-colored lips pouty. "Are you coming? We've all got our swimsuits!" She held up a minuscule scrap of material, twirling it teas-

113

ingly over her head, and giggled. Her rowdy friends agreed loudly.

"Go ahead," Jordan said. "I'll be there in a minute."

The car spun away, flinging gravel, and Kat's heart sank. She stood frozen. Jordan cast her a dubious glance. "Just some people over for drinks and a swim," he explained. "Come on. I'll round up those breeding records and you can have a drink with us. There's probably an extra swimsuit around somewhere, too."

But Kat was no masochist. "I think I'll pass this time. I —I just remembered I have to get some proofs to Leann," she supplied by way of explanation. It was true enough, and as convenient an excuse as any.

Jordan's look of comprehension held just an element of relief. "Well, if you're certain you won't . . ."

"Not this time, thanks." She forced a smile. "I'm too whipped to be sociable anyway. I'll give that name some thought."

"Sure."

They parted and each headed toward home, both wishing they were going anywhere else in the world.

"No, don't you dare bring them over tonight!" Leann ordered through the telephone receiver when Kat called several hours later. "Both girls have a stomach bug that I wouldn't wish on my worst enemy!"

"Oh, Leann. Is there any way I can help?"

Freshly showered and dressed in a comfortable cotton caftan, Kat felt up to anything. She grimaced against a tiny stab of jealous pain and mentally revised her estimation. Anything but dealing with the fact that Jordan was probably at this very minute cavorting with Sondra. Even sick room duty was better than *that*.

"You're a love, but no, we've got it under control," Leann said. "Give us a day or two, okay?"

"Sure, but I can't wait until you see the pictures of your

beautiful girls." Kat laughed. "You'll forgive them anything, including a stomach virus, when you see how ador-
able they look. Having the world's greatest photographer at
work didn't hurt, either."

"Such modesty!"

"No brag, just fact." Kat laughed. She kicked at the
telephone cord which was long enough to reach any room
in the house, straightening it out around the leg of the
kitchen table. She cocked the receiver between her ear and
shoulder and picked up a glossy proof in each hand. Com-
paring the shots, she discarded one, riffled through the
stack and selected another. Leann's cherubs smiled up at
her from each photograph. "Your main problem will be
deciding which one you like best," she promised her friend
cheerfully.

"I can't wait to see them. By the way," Leann asked,
"how did the McElroys like the wedding pictures?"

"They were pleased, and ordered quite a few over the
package deal. I hope I get more bookings because of
them."

"Have—have you gotten any response to your ad in the
paper?" Leann asked, a hesitant note in her voice.

"No, and I'm a bit surprised, but I suppose that summer
is kind of slow. After all, school's out, and my getting the
McElroy wedding was really a fluke." Kat frowned.
"What's the matter, Leann? I have the feeling you're not
telling me something."

She heard a gusty sigh on the other end of the line. "I
don't really know whether to tell you this or not . . ."

"Tell me what?"

"Well, Don's mother heard it from a friend, and she
knew you and I were friends, and so she wanted to know,
but of course, I told her it was ridiculous and tried to
explain—"

"Explain what?" Kat asked, exasperated.

"That you're a very good photographer, the tops, and

115

anything Mrs. Scott is saying to her friends about you is sheer rubbish!"

"Oh. I might have known." Kat's words were without inflection.

"The question is, what are we going to do about it?"

"There's nothing to do. She's never liked me."

"I know, but this is weird, like she's really out to get you or something. Saying mean things about your work and whether you should even be around children. It's ridiculous! Why would she want to hurt your photography business like that?"

"Use your head, Leann," Kat said tiredly. "What better way to drive me away from her precious son? If I can't make a living in Mansfield I'll have to go elsewhere."

"But you work for Jordan now!"

"Just temporarily. She can't do anything about that without making Jordan wonder, so she's trying a little character assassination. I'm only surprised it took her this long."

"Well, we can fix *her* little red wagon!" Leann said indignantly. "I'll tell Don's mother and—"

"No, Leann, I'm not going to try to fight something as insidious as a whisper campaign. People will believe what they want."

"Katherine Holt! It's not like you to give up so easily," Leann admonished.

Kat rested her forehead on her hand and sighed. "I don't know, Leann. Sometimes I wonder if I was quite in my right mind to come back to Mansfield. Maybe I should have stayed overseas." Images of death on the blitzed streets of Beirut, captured forever through the square of a viewfinder, crowded through her brain. She rubbed the fading scar on her shoulder. "No, I take that back," she said abruptly. "It has been good for me, in ways I can't begin to explain."

"And Jordan?"

116

"Is Jordan. Don't get your hopes up in that department," Kat said wryly. Only behind self-mockery could she hide her growing despondency.

"Well, we can do something about this photography career of yours!" Leann replied stoutly. "I'll put my thinking cap on and see what I can come up with. Just wait until I show my girls' pictures around town, too. There will be people beating down your door."

"You're a good friend. I feel better just knowing you're on the job." There was a knock on the front door. "I'll let you go, Leann. Someone's here." She hung up and walked through the living room to find Jordan on the other side of the screen door.

"Well, Katherine, aren't you going to invite me in?" he asked. At her hesitation, his eyebrow lifted in sardonic amusement, almost meeting the damp lock of coffee brown hair falling across his forehead.

Kat pushed open the door. "Aren't you neglecting your guests?"

"They've gone," he replied with a shrug. "Not that they needed a host anyway."

He moved restlessly, scanning the room, remembering, noting the changes Kat's return had made. Photographic catalogs lay scattered on the tables. A pair of her sandals poked toe-first from under the threadbare sofa. On the old metal desk neatly labeled rolls of film stood in rows between her Rolleiflex and Nikon.

Kat pondered his words curiously. "Was there something you wanted?"

He seemed to remember where he was. "Oh. Yeah. I brought you a copy of those breeding records." He dug in his shorts pocket and pulled out a piece of paper, passing it to Kat.

"I don't think I'll need it." She glanced at the paper then back to Jordan, her lips quirking upward.

"Why? Have you come up with a name already?"

117

"I think so. But you aren't going to like it."

"Maybe I'd better sit down then." He grinned and threw himself down on the creaky old sofa, long legs outstretched, his fingers laced together at the back of his neck. "Okay, let me have it."

Kat laughed softly. "Do you remember what Bertie used to say whenever one of us acted badly or threw a temper tantrum?"

"Uh-uh." He shook his head and his grin grew more lopsided.

"She'd say that we'd 'cut a rusty.' So—Cutta Rusty, after his sire, Calcutta, and his owner, Rusty."

"Hmm." Jordan's eyelids drooped to half-mast and he looked thoughtful.

"I knew you wouldn't like it." She swung away, but Jordan was faster, catching her hand and pulling her down beside him on the couch.

"Who says I don't like it?" he demanded.

"Then you do? Is it really okay?" Her voice was slightly breathless, and her skin tingled where his hand met hers.

"Very clever. And appropriate." He chuckled. "Maybe we should mark the occasion of our agreement with a celebratory drink?"

"Iced tea with lemon?"

"You haven't forgotten."

"Not likely, as many gallons of the stuff as I've seen you put away," she said with a laugh. "I'll get it."

"I'll help."

In the kitchen Kat reached into the cupboard for glasses and Jordan paused curiously at the table. With a cautious fingertip he examined the photographs.

"Don and Leann's girls," he said. He looked up as Kat filled the glasses with ice and lemon, then poured the tea. "You're good. Damn good."

"Thanks." She handed him a glass. "They were good subjects."

Ignoring the glass in his hand, Jordan reached for another picture, smiling at Leslie's cherubic grin captured in the glossy eight-by-ten. "Cute kids," he murmured, then his eyes fell on another print unearthed by his shufflings. He picked it up and his glance flicked toward Kat, then back. She leaned closer to see which one he had, then flushed. It was Jordan holding Leslie, love and affection shining on both faces.

"That's a good picture of you, Jordan," Kat said. "You're very photogenic, like your dad was. The senator was the camera's darling."

"Is that the only reason you took this?" There was a strange note in his voice. He took a slow pull from the dewy glass, then set it down.

"Well, no. The expressions, the . . ." She trailed off, took the print from him and studied it. Her voice was low. "You're a man who should have children, Jordan."

"It might have happened. Do you ever think about that? We took a lot of chances together, you and I."

Kat's heart thumped heavily against the wall of her chest. She couldn't look at him. "We were very foolish, or just plain crazy."

"Crazy in love. Things might have been very different for us if you had gotten pregnant."

"Different, yes. But who can say if it would have been better or worse?" She looked up into his eyes, saw the strange, haunted light in them, knew that his "what if's" had been the same as hers during all the long years apart.

"We might have a child ten years old right now if we had been lucky—or unlucky."

"We'd have had to move to Australia," she said, but her laugh was unsteady. She shook her head and swallowed. "Neither of our families would have been able to accept it."

"Australia wouldn't have been so bad." He reached out,

his fingertips brushing her cheek, her earlobe, setting the dangling gold loop to swinging.

"No, it wouldn't." She shivered at his touch, then stepped back, hoping he hadn't felt the betraying tremor. Her hands were damp from the sweat on her tea glass. Turning, she ripped off a paper towel from a roll on the counter and folded it around the glass. With her back turned, she continued. "Why haven't you married and had a family, Jordan? It certainly can't be for lack of opportunity."

"Are you referring to Sondra?"

Kat swung around, shrugging. She lifted the glass to her lips and peered over its rim at him. "For lack of another name."

"She's just a kid."

"Quite a pretty one. Fun, too, I'm sure." Kat couldn't understand why she was being so perverse. Asking these questions was like picking at a tender scab on a half-healed wound.

"Sure." Jordan's eyes darkened. "But I can't imagine spending the rest of my life with her."

Kat's breath seeped from her lungs, a singing relief trilling deep in her heart. But still she sought reassurance. "Bertie says your mother would welcome her as a daughter-in-law. And you're bound to produce a flock of red-haired offspring."

"You're awfully concerned with me siring children," Jordan said. "I've told you I'm not interested in Sondra, so what gives, Kat?" He advanced upon her, pinning her against the cabinet and taking her glass from her suddenly nerveless fingers. He trailed his fingers down her throat to where her pulse skipped rapidly in the hollow of her neck, and his voice was husky. "Are you volunteering for the job?"

"I—I'm not sure I'd meet your qualifications," Kat an-

120

swered with a nervous laugh. She bit her lip and unconsciously raised her fingers to toy with her earring.

"Forget long-term requirements. I'm willing to try a probationary period." He batted her fingers away from her ear, then carefully unclasped her earring. He tossed it on the counter behind her.

Kat trembled at this intimate task. She bit back a gasp when he leaned forward, nipping at her earlobe with his teeth, then nuzzling the slope of her neck. "Jordan, please . . ." Her murmur was choked, and she wasn't even sure what she asked of him.

Jordan's lips found hers, warm, soft, persuasive. His tongue parted her lips, then he was inside her mouth, sweet and potent and lemony. Kat felt dizzy, all her strength sapped by the power of his kiss. Her heart swelled to the bursting point with all the love she felt for this man. Here was her haven, her home, only in his arms, lost in his kiss. Surely he knew, surely he could feel it? How simple to say the words, yet how vulnerable it would make her!

Jordan lifted his head and Kat drew in a shaky breath. Somehow her hands had found their way around his neck. Her voice wobbled. "Is this a seduction, counselor?"

"It could be," he rumbled. "Perhaps if we adjourn . . . ?" He nodded in the direction of her bedroom.

Kat swallowed. He was making it her choice. Later there would be no way she could say she was swept away. Her body ached with wanting him, yet she held back. Was he offering more than just physical release? Body language was inadmissible evidence. Testimony was what she needed from this lawyer—what she had to have.

"I think the jury is still out on this one," she said slowly, lowering her hands.

A mask of indifference seemed to drop over Jordan's expression and he released her. "Just exactly what is it you want, Katherine?"

"I want more than a one-night stand with you, Jordan,"

she said earnestly. "Especially with you. I need the words."

"It would be just that—just words. I can't give you what you want."

"And I can't settle for less," she whispered, her lower lip quivering. "Not this time."

"I wasn't the one who made that decision before."

Frustration bubbled up within Kat. If he only knew . . . but no, there was no use in that. When would he learn that recriminations were pointless? They had to go on from here and now, but again Jordan remained stuck in the past. A cloud of discouragement settled over Kat.

"Then I guess the verdict is in. Neither one of us is able to give the other anything. Hung jury. I'm sorry, Jordan."

He studied her for a long moment. "I'll let myself out," he said at last. He turned away, then stopped at her husky rendering of his old name.

"Rusty?" she quavered, refusing to douse the final glimmer of hope. "I'll be here—if the court reverses its decision."

Someone pounding on the front door awakened her. She recognized Jordan's voice immediately, and for a fleeting, semiconscious moment she thought he had come to her with the commitment she wanted. But the tone of his voice held something else, something worried and desperate.

Scrubbing the traces of tears from her cheeks with her knuckles, Kat crawled out of bed, banging her toe on the phone she'd taken off the hook to be undisturbed in her misery.

"I'm coming!" she called, pulling her hair back, stumbling in the dark to the front door.

Jordan wasted no time with greetings. His face was gaunt and stubbled in the yellow porch light. "Get dressed.

We've got two really sick foals. The vet's coming and I need you."

Unquestioningly, Kat moved at once. Riding beside him back to the farm, she reflected sadly that need was always a relative term.

CHAPTER EIGHT

Sometimes it got so a man couldn't tell where reality ended and the nightmare began, Jordan thought. It was the end of the second week of fighting a deadly, microscopic organism that attacked the young foals swiftly, with lethal results. Grainy eyes and a mind in a perpetual daze was only part of the price he paid as days and nights faded together.

Jordan sat in his kitchen and stared at the sandwich Bertie placed before him, too dispirited to eat. For two hellish weeks they had battled for the lives of the sick babies with a hospital's technology. With IVs and Ringer's solutions, blood counts and stomach lavage. They had worked around the clock, combating the vicious cycle of dehydration, severe diarrhea, colic, and stomach ulcers; worked against time, against the demands of the body.

Everyone had to eat when they could, but he only poked at the sandwich, too tired to care. Even the shower he'd taken hadn't helped much. He felt guilty about neglecting his work at the office, but his secretary was coping. And anyway, how could he concentrate on anything but the mysterious sickness?

He couldn't clear his mind of the picture of once frisky colts pawing the ground, rolling in agony, unable to nurse or drink, then stoically submitting to whatever horrors the vet inflicted on them in the search for a cure. He couldn't shake the vision of their eyes, wide and frightened, despite

Kat's gentle hands and soothing voice. Thank God for her. The others, too. He couldn't have asked for more devotion from any of them.

He pushed the sandwich aside and dug into his shirt pocket for a slip of paper. The blood tests had finally identified the sickness. It was a rotavirus. Where the hell had it come from?

He crumpled the lab slip and threw it down on the table. It didn't matter. They had no choice but to vaccinate the whole herd, even though it would be too late for the little ones. He pinched the bridge of his nose tiredly. Maybe they'd reached a turning point. There hadn't been any new cases among the foals in two days and the rest seemed to be holding their own now. If things just held together for a while . . .

There was a knock on the kitchen door. As Bertie opened the door for J.W., Jordan got to his feet.

"What is it, J.W.?"

"We just lost another one. The vet said his stomach ruptured."

"Jesus!" Jordan ran a hand through his hair. Another one, despite all their efforts! He sighed. "I'll go talk to the doctor."

"Uh, that's not all."

"What else?" Jordan demanded.

"It's Lady Sabrina's colt. Looks like he's got it, too."

Jordan fought for control as rage and frustration and a terrible foreboding flooded through him.

Damn! Not Cutta Rusty!

"Did I carry it to him, Jordan?" Kat's wan face was tortured. "I was so careful . . ."

"Don't blame yourself. It came from out of nowhere." They watched the listless colt, his head hanging. *Why did it have to be this one?* Jordan thought wretchedly, *Kat's favorite.* "We're going to have to pump his stomach again."

"Oh, no. Not again. He's so weak."

Her eyes were pale in her washed-out countenance, like two chips of blue ice. Dark purple shadows formed half moons of fatigue under her eyes. She was so tired. They all were. But Kat was a trooper, he'd give her that. She hadn't complained once, no matter how nasty or unpleasant the task. A tender affection and admiration welled within him for the tired woman at his side. Even with every trace of prettiness wiped from her face by exhaustion, she was still beautiful. Inside, where it really counted. Why hadn't he realized it before? Or had he simply forgotten? And they'd won, beaten that damned virus. All except for this one.

"We don't have a choice," he said gruffly. "J.W. and I will do it when the vet gets here. I want you to go home and get some sleep."

"I'm okay."

"Do what I say, Kat."

"I'll find a place to nap, but I won't go home," she said stubbornly. "I've got a right, haven't I?"

She had a point, and he knew it. More right than any-body, really. Slowly, he nodded. "All right."

"You'll wake me if I'm needed, won't you?"

"Yes."

She stumbled off toward the makeshift bunk of hay and blankets they'd set up in an empty stall. Jordan watched her go, then turned back to Cutta Rusty with a growing sense of dread.

"Katherine. Wake up, sweetheart."

Kat struggled up out of the mire of exhaustion, fighting the glue that held her eyelids together. What . . . She sat up suddenly, blinking. Hay rustled beneath her and she could smell the musty stale odor of the woolen blankets. Jordan squatted beside her, his face grim.

"What?" she muttered. Jordan didn't say anything. She glanced at him, saw the unusual pasty color beneath his

126

tan, and panic surged through her. "What is it? What's happened?" She tried to get up but Jordan's hands held her.

"The vet was here."

"And?" Kat saw him swallow.

"I made the decision. We had to put the colt down."

"What? No," she denied on a shaky laugh. "He wasn't that sick."

"He was suffering terribly. It came on fast at the end."

"No! Let me see!" she cried. She pushed to her feet, trying to shrug out of Jordan's grip, but he held her firmly, his mouth compressed in a tight line.

"It's all over, Kat. He's gone. J.W.'s taking Sabrina out now."

"You bastard! You said you'd call me! I could have saved him!" she screamed. She struggled wildly, her eyes bright with angry tears.

"Kat, please—"

His words were interrupted by a shrill scream from the mare. Suddenly, all hell broke loose. Sabrina kicked and reared, J.W. shouted, the other men's voices added to the commotion. The blind mare's shrieks as she refused to leave her baby were ear-splitting. Kat flew at Jordan in a frenzy to be free.

"Kat! Pull yourself together!" Jordan snapped, giving her a shake. "I've got to go help them with Sabrina. Stay here, do you understand?"

Numbly, Kat nodded. Jordan released her and ran to lend a hand with the frantic mare. They led the horse away. Kat watched the men move around. The vet left the stall. Then Pete and Jimbo came out, carrying the dead colt between them. They lugged the body to the waiting pickup and swung it into the bed of the truck. It landed with a sickening thud and a tinkling jingle of silver bell. The mare's screams peaked, dwindled, then began again.

Kat clapped her hands over her ears and squeezed her

127

eyes shut. Giant shudders racked her. Hot, scalding tears slipped down her cheeks. Body wagons were an everyday sight on the streets of Beirut. Mothers keened dirges for loved ones somewhere every minute of every hour. Even people you knew, friends you loved, could die. Sabrina shrieked again, broke away from the men and came galloping back toward the stall.

Something shattered inside Kat as great sobs tore through her. She bolted, hands still pressed to her ears. Escape. Through the barn, across the starlit pasture, down through the dark woods, up onto the porch, to burst into her own familiar living room, her sides heaving. But it wasn't enough. Papa John wasn't there anymore to hold her until the terror went away. And Bill was gone, her friend with the lovely sensitive poetry and wife waiting at home. Even a baby horse with a rusty coat. She was alone again.

A primitive urge to hurt something back made her pick up a glass ashtray and send it hurtling against the far wall. A sweep of her arm and the books fell like lifeless birds from the bookshelves. Sobbing hoarsely, she picked up the next thing her fingers fell on.

"Kat, no!" Jordan plucked the camera from Kat's hands, ignoring her scream of rage. He placed it safely on the desk and reached for her. She backed away, her breath sobbing from her lungs, eyes wide and teary, fear and anger battling for control.

"Get away from me!" she shouted, her hair flying, her eyes wild with the crazed light of an animal in pain. "You —you murderer!"

"Kat, try to understand." Jordan was white around the mouth, in torment at her anguish. He couldn't believe that his strong, valiant Kat was on the verge of hysteria. He felt so helpless.

"I hate you!" She backed against a table, felt for something—anything—then hurled the book at Jordan, catch-

128

ing him above his right eyebrow. With a yell, he jumped at her, caught her shoulders and shook her.

"Kat, that's enough!"

Kat froze, her breath coming in hiccups. She stared at the trickle of blood on Jordan's forehead for an everlasting moment, then her face crumpled.

"Oh, no," she moaned, her head lolling forward. "Even you. Everything I touch turns to death and destruction."

"Honey, it's all right. I'm not hurt."

But she seemed not to understand his words. Suddenly, it was all pouring out of her, all the horror of Bill's death, how she hadn't been able to help him, either. How she'd failed, so miserably, and how she hadn't even had the decency to die, too. Guilt and failure, disappointment after disappointment. And then the colt. Everything she loved turned out a disaster. Everything.

Jordan gathered her in his arms and let her sob out her sorrows on his broad chest. He held her close to his heart, feet braced to support her, and felt the sobs wrack her slim body as the anguish overwhelmed her. He swallowed harshly on the clog in his throat, the moisture in his own eyes, and buried his chin in her hair. She smelled of clean air and hay and woman.

Oh, Kat, how did we come to this?

His shirt was sodden with her tears when he finally lifted her and carried her to the bedroom. She was limp and uncharacteristically docile when he undressed her down to her underwear, then wiped her swollen eyes with a cool cloth and tucked her into the old iron bed.

He returned the cloth to the bathroom, then came and sat down beside her.

"Better?" he asked gently. She nodded, calmer now, the sheet drawn up to her chin.

"I'm such an ass."

Her words brought a smile. "On occasion." He picked

up her limp hand and massaged the back of it with the flat of his thumb.

"I'm sorry," she said. Her bottom lip trembled.

"That was quite a pile of garbage you unloaded. You've been carrying around a lot of nonsense for too long, Kat. Are you going to be all right?"

She swallowed hard. She was far from all right. She was raw and vulnerable and needed his love to fight off the demons. "N-no."

"Aw, kitten . . ." He reached for her and she was in his arms, shuddering violently.

"Hold me, Jordan. Keep me safe." She clung to him, her face pressed against his strong body.

Her words wrenched at Jordan's soul. He made soothing noises deep in his throat and stroked her hair back from her flushed forehead with tender fingers. The shudders subsided gradually, replaced by a subtle, yet growing awareness. He cupped her cheeks in his palms and used his thumbs to tilt her face upward. They searched each other's eyes for a long, tremulous moment, uncertain, almost shy.

Jordan's caramel gaze dropped to her lips. Slowly, hesitantly, his mouth followed, brushing hers with a feathery caress.

"I can't be your knight on a white horse, kitten," he said, his voice husky and low. "I'm just a man."

"It's not the dream, or even the memory I love, Jordan. It's you. It's always been you."

A bolt of something bold and jubilant and terrifying scorched him. "Kat . . ."

"Hush," she said, placing her fingertips on his lips and shaking her head. "I love you. And I want whatever you can give. Now. Not yesterday. Not tomorrow. Now."

"It may not be enough for you." His eyes narrowed in warning, a chilling reflection of the old, harsh Jordan.

But Kat had made her decision, or perhaps it had been

made for her, forged by time and experience and the knowledge of what was necessary to her very existence. Her fingers traveled to the back of his head, threaded through his thick hair, pulled him closer until his lips were only a whisper away.

"It's enough."

Their lips met, melded, and instantly lost their innocence. Jordan pulled her hard against him, a low moan rumbling deep in his chest, a sound of raw male sexual hunger that inflamed Kat's senses. He rolled slightly, pulling her half across his lap, and deepened the kiss, plundering her mouth for her honeyed secrets. The sheet dropped away and his hand slipped under her bra strap in back, kneading her pliant flesh, then deftly unhooked the bit of nylon. A crooked finger caught one shoulder strap and eased it sideways. His mouth moved to follow its path and Kat arched her neck, allowing him access.

Jordan pulled back to slip the garment down her arms. Kat assisted eagerly, hunching her shoulders forward while her fingers worked at the buttons of Jordan's shirt. The bra dropped unheeded to the floor. She sat up, tugging the tail of his shirt from his jeans. His hands roamed down her arms and captured her wrists, holding them still.

Kat's eyes flicked up to Jordan's face, but his gaze rested on her breasts. Her breath caught. His eyes moved over her in a searing, tangible caress and her breasts tingled, became heavy and swollen under his heated regard.

"Beautiful," he murmured. "So beautiful." He raised both hands to cup the rounded, creamy globes, weighing the sweet flesh, brushing the crowns with his thumbs. Her rosy nipples tightened into peaked buds and Kat moaned softly.

"Oh, Rusty, it's been so long," she whispered, her lashes fanning down.

Gently, he eased her back onto the bed, stripped off his shirt, and pressed down on top of her, their mouths coming together with growing urgency. His leg moved between her thighs and Kat felt the hard proof of his desire against her.

Sensation poured through Kat like fine red wine, hearty and intoxicating. Memories of other times, other places with him rushed in, swirling together with the immediate reality of Jordan's lovemaking, forceful, mature, intensely masculine. Then the memories faded as reality exploded with new excitement, merging the sweetness of a shared past to make the present rapture infinitely better, a vernal communion of souls and bodies.

Jordan wooed her tongue with his, stroking, probing, dueling in the primitive mating ritual that echoed the one to come. Kat met his demands with abandon, her love spilling out of her heart to wash away all doubts, all hesitations. She wanted to give and give until she was as empty of reservations as last harvest's flagon and filled to the brim with the heady spring wine of desire. This is what she had been made for, to find oblivion and peace and surging excitement in this man's arms.

Her hands moved feverishly over him, pressing the hard muscles of his back, slipping beneath the waistband of his jeans to trace the hollows at the base of his spine. She could feel the springlike tension in him, rejoiced at the involuntary shudders her seeking hands provoked. Her fingers slipped around to the front of his jeans, fumbled with the belt buckle, traced the outline of snap and zipper.

Jordan groaned, jerked his mouth free and grabbed her hands, bringing them up to his chest. "Good God, woman! What are you trying to do to me?" He leaned over her and his breathing was ragged. A bemused, lopsided grin creased his cheek.

"To touch you." Her eyes were wide, deep blue with passion. Her fingers curled into the thatch of soft black hairs on his chest, her nails delicately scraping his taut male nipples. He sucked in a breath and bared his soul.

"You do touch me, in places no one else could ever

reach." He lowered his head and trailed a path of fire down the valley between her breasts, then traveled across one snowy mound to tease and tickle the peak with his tongue.

Kat gasped and arched, bringing her closer to Jordan's special magic. He laved the sensitive area with his tongue, then took the whole nipple into his mouth to suckle gently. A taut wire strummed from her breasts to her belly, melting and liquefying all the moist secret places. He moved to the other breast and Kat cried out, clutching his shoulders in a spasm of excitement and need. She tugged his jaw, finding his lips with hers, murmuring her need and love against his mouth over and over.

Jordan pulled away to shed his garments eagerly, then pulled the last scrap of fabric away from her hips and gathered her close. Side by side, they relearned each other's bodies, hands caressing, legs entwined, mouths locked until, gasping, they pulled apart to draw in ragged breaths.

Fingers explored the planes and angles of the other's face; the tilt of jawbone, the arch of eyebrow, the silky texture of hair, the sensitive bow of lips well kissed. They paused at a quiet plateau, midway on their journey to ecstasy, sharing secret smiles and the knowledge that the pleasure they found in each other was only beginning.

"I want you, kitten," Jordan rasped against her ear. "God, how I want you!"

"Then love me, Jordan, love me now."

He rolled over her and she took the heated velvety shaft, guiding him, arching to meet him, clasping his hard length deep inside her in a joining so sweet and rich she cried out with joy. And each deep thrust, each strong, sliding probe was a paean of life and love, and she rose to meet him, giving him everything, holding nothing in reserve, emptying her soul with her words.

"I love you, love you, *love you.*"

And there was nothing left within to interfere with the sensuous, culminating spasms, the overpowering contractions of mindless release that pitched her blindly over the precipice, soaring in his arms while he spilled himself into her and called her name.

And the sensation was like no other, leaving her boneless, satiated, cleansed of anxiety and guilt, so that she fell, dreamless, into the welcome well of sleep still joined to his body.

Kat heard the first bird chirpings, recognized the heralds of dawn, but refused to open her eyes. She felt so content, so full of well-being, drifting on that level between sleep and true wakefulness. She felt truly rested, energized, and she moved sensuously, realizing that she was naked under the cool cotton sheet. A formless question made a tiny pucker in her brow. She opened her eyes.

Jordan.

He half lay on a pile of pillows propped against the iron headboard, his hands laced together behind his head, gazing thoughtfully off into the distance. Curled on her side, arm under her ear, Kat watched him covertly. The sheet covered him to the waist, but his broad chest lay stretched out for her inspection, each muscle delineated, the whorls of black hair trailing down his flat stomach. A morning stubble shadowed his jaw and his coffee-colored hair fell over his forehead, almost hiding the little notched vee of dried blood where the book had hit him. He was brown and big and very male—and in her bed. Kat felt her mouth go dry, startled by the intensity of renewed desire.

Maybe he felt her sudden tension. He turned his head and saw her looking at him. She smiled, half good-morning, half invitation.

"Hi." Her voice was husky, tentative.

"Katherine." Slowly, Jordan unlaced his fingers, then rolled to his side and propped on his elbow, head in hand, gazing down into her sleepy and love-softened face. Kat blinked at his solemn expression. He reached out with the other hand, idly spreading her tangled honey-blond hair against the pillow, a few of the silky strands clinging to the rough skin on his palm. "You're very beautiful."

"Thank you." Kat felt confused. He'd paid her the compliment with all the inflection he would have used in saying "fire is hot." A chill of premonition cooled her blood. Was Jordan regretting what had happened already?

"And extremely desirable." He lowered his head and his mouth covered hers. Kat felt dizzy when he stopped kissing her. "And very passionate."

"Is—is something wrong?"

"Why did you walk out on me eleven years ago?"

Kat opened her mouth to answer and found she couldn't. She couldn't meet his eyes. Rolling over, she sat up with her back to him, partially wrapped in the rumpled sheet, her feet dangling. She pushed a shaky hand through her hair and glanced back over her shoulder.

"I—I've got to get to the farm. Do you want coffee?"

His hand snaked out to grab her wrist. "J.W. will take care of it, and no, I don't want any damn coffee. I want an answer!"

"Jordan, please. I don't know what you want me to say." She sighed. "We've been over this before."

"I know. I've been over and over it in my mind for hours, lying here beside you listening to you breathe. It just doesn't add up. All these years wasted. You robbed us, Katherine. I want to know why."

She turned toward him, her shackled hand lying between them. Her expression was troubled, earnest. "Jordan, I love you. What's done can't be undone. It doesn't matter anymore. Can't we go on from here?"

"I hated you, did you know that?"

She jerked in shock. His expression hardened with remembered pain and unanswerable questions.

"You stuck a knife in my guts and sent me to a living hell. It didn't take me long to learn it was better not to feel

135

at all." His fingers tightened bruisingly on her wrist. "Was it the trial? Or the families? Or did you just stop loving me?"

"It was more complicated than that," she began desperately. How could she tell him? Was it finally time? If she told him the truth now about his mother's part in the death of their love affair, would he even believe her? On the cusp of indecision, Kat hesitated.

"How complicated? Tell me, Kat."

"Your mother—" She broke off the explanation abruptly. No, it wasn't right to build her own happiness by destroying another's. And since Jordan's was inexorably linked with hers, to reveal a nasty picture of a mother he loved would only make matters worse.

"What about her?"

"Your parents—it was just too hard on them. I . . . I knew how much you loved them, and I didn't want you to have to make a choice between us. I thought later . . ." She shrugged. "Well, things don't always work out just because you want them to." She tugged at her hand.

Jordan released her. "So you made the noble sacrifice? Now why do I find that so hard to believe?" he asked mildly.

She nearly laughed at his phrasing. Sacrifice didn't half describe what she had done. But the laughter was too bitter to release. She offered words instead. "It's hard to know your mind when you're only seventeen. I thought I was doing the right thing for everybody."

"Free-spirited Kat Holt, setting the world on its ear. Why don't you just admit you had a change of heart? Was there another man?"

"No!" she exclaimed, aghast. "Oh, Jordan, how could you even think such a thing?" A tiny angry blaze shone in her eyes. She jerked the sheet around her and stalked to the dresser, pulling clothing from drawers and slamming them shut with unnecessary force.

"I never knew what to think. I still don't," he said quietly. He eased his long, rangy length out of bed and strode up behind her, nude and magnificent. He grasped her shoulders, pinning her reflection with his eyes in the age-spotted mirror over the dresser.

Kat saw the tangled blond image of herself superimposed over his darker, male outline. His hard, tanned fingers pressed into the paler, softer skin of her shoulders. Warm breath stirred the strands of hair at her ear.

"You didn't wait around to find out I had already made my choice," he said. "I came to your birthday party with a ring in my pocket, Kat."

"Ohhh." The sound was a moan of sheer pain. She whirled to face him, clutching the sheet and clothes in a ball at her breasts. "I can't take any of it back!" she cried. "Aren't you ever going to forgive me? What about what we have now? Doesn't it mean anything at all?"

"What exactly do we have, Katherine?" His voice was angry, sardonic. "How do I know I'm not getting drawn into another self-destructive situation? You made promises before that you didn't keep."

"I'll keep them this time," she said desperately.

"How can I be sure? Let's face it. You needed a shoulder to cry on last night and I was convenient. It was good sex, but that's all it was."

"That's a lie." Her raw whisper was filled with pain. How could he deny the beauty of what they had shared?

His eyes trailed reluctantly, insultingly over the rounded curves revealed by the sagging sheet. "You're what the legal profession calls an 'attractive nuisance.' I knew better than to let you get too close. It won't happen again."

She went rigid with hurt. Her lips barely moved. "Get out."

He stared at her set face. "Yeah, maybe it is time I left," he drawled.

"Get out!"

He picked up his jeans, stepped into them, then gathered his other clothing and left.

The screen door on the porch slammed shut behind him. Kat slumped as the sound echoed through the house and a hot tear slid down her cheek. Losing Jordan once was hard enough. Losing him twice was unbearable.

CHAPTER NINE

"You ain't a-goin' to win her standing here mooning after her, boy."

Jordan started slightly at Bertie's acerbic statement. His lips curled in self-mockery. That was exactly what he'd been doing, standing in front of the living-room window watching the barn, hoping for another glimpse of Kat's distant silhouette. It had been a grueling day at the office, everything demanding immediate attention because of his neglect during the epidemic. He'd come home wrung dry, and he certainly hadn't expected to find Kat at the farm, not after last night and this morning. But she'd come to work just as though nothing had happened. Stubborn woman!

The sun ducked behind a gray cloud, and he turned away from the window.

"Your vivid imagination always astounds me, Bertie," he murmured. The ice in his glass of Jack Daniel's tinkled softly. He took a sip, letting the fiery liquor burn down his throat, hoping it would somehow anesthetize the ache in his gut.

Bertie snorted. "Don't you use them two-dollar words with me! I got eyes. I know when a bed's been slept in or not. But you know I never say anything!"

Jordan stared down into the amber depths of his glass and restrained a smile. "Of course not."

"Don't you get sassy with me. I've tanned your bottom plenty of times, and I'm liable to again if you don't straighten out whatever's wrong between you and Kat."

"She doesn't want it straightened out."

"Horsefeathers! Any fool can see she's crazy in love with you. Seems to me you're the one's got to decide what you want."

"I wish it were that simple," he muttered. It was impossible to know what he wanted when his loins screamed "yes," his brain shouted "no," and his heart was so mixed up it sang and cried at the same time.

"If you've got any sense at all, you'll go down there and at least offer that child a ride home. Can't you see it's coming up a rainstorm?"

Jordan glanced out the window. A few large drops splashed into the hot dust on the driveway. There was a distant, faraway rumble of thunder.

How much sense did it make to fight a compulsion he knew in the end he could never resist? The knowledge that Kat was near drew him inexorably back to her. Was she his salvation or his destruction? There was only one way to find out.

He set the glass on a nearby table and dropped a swift kiss on Bertie's wrinkled cheek. "You're right. Thanks."

He left the house with a jingle of keys, the door slamming shut behind him just as the phone rang. With a little sigh of annoyance, Bertie bustled over to pick up the receiver.

"Hello? Oh, hello, Mrs. Scott. No, he isn't here." Bertie was careful to keep the satisfaction out of her voice. "I don't know when to expect him back. He's gone out with Kat Holt."

"I don't want a ride."

"Nonsense. You'll be drenched. Bertie's orders."

Kat stared at Jordan suspiciously, defiance and wounded

140

pride filling her. What did this man want from her? She bit the inside of her lip to keep it from trembling. She would not cry again. She flipped her hair over her shoulder and smoothed the flaming red shirt she'd thrown over her jeans to prove she was a survivor.

"No, thank you." The words were scarcely out of her mouth before the summer thunderstorm released its power. Kat stood at the entrance to the barn and watched the white sheets of rain lash the thirsty ground, trying not to think of a new grave in the woods where the horse cemetery was located. Sabrina was grieving in her own way, nickering forlornly for a colt and a tinkling bell that never came.

The fresh smell of rain collided with the odor of dry earth and Kat inhaled deeply. She was conscious of Jordan behind her, watching the rain, too. His voice was low when he spoke.

"J.W. thinks the mares we sent to Kentucky brought the virus back. I think he's right."

"Can you prove it?"

"No. But it's changed our procedures. We'll quarantine returning mares, and vaccinate differently. With any luck, we'll never have to go through this again."

"Good."

"Come on, Katherine," he persuaded gently. "It's not letting up. No use getting soaked."

Kat measured the unrelenting rainfall with a practiced eye and sighed. He was right. Although what he hoped to accomplish was beyond her. Her calm façade was as fragile as a soap bubble, and just as fleeting under his presence and surprising show of thoughtfulness. She was mystified at his sudden behavior; after this morning she would have sworn that he didn't want to see her again. But he had sought her out deliberately. Just when she thought she knew right where she stood, the earth slid under her feet

141

and left her floundering again. She had neither the energy nor the will to fight him.

"All right."

The dash to his car left her damp and breathless, which was just as well since she didn't have a word to say. She merely stared morosely out of the moisture-fogged window as he drove down the driveway.

"You look tired," Jordan remarked. Kat flashed him a glance that labeled his words at best inept, at worst tasteless, considering the circumstances. He continued, apparently unconcerned at her glower. "When was the last time you ate?"

"Oh, really, Jordan. Spare me," she snapped in growing irritation.

"Which means probably not at all today," he returned smoothly. "Burgers okay? Nobody makes them like Ryberg's."

Kat gaped at him, then gasped when he drove past the turn into her drive, continuing on the road into Mansfield.

"I can't take this," she muttered in a strained voice. "Turn this thing around and take me home."

"Kat, we need to talk."

"Talk?" Her laugh was harsh. "I think you just about said it all this morning!"

"Maybe . . . maybe I was wrong."

The swish of the windshield wipers was rhythmic and too loud in the silent car. Stunned, Kat sat frozen while her heart drummed wildly. At length, she gave a little moan and buried her face in her hands, bending into her lap as though she were in pain.

"Don't do this. Please, Jordan," she said, her words muffled. "Don't build up my hopes just to dash them down again."

With a subdued oath, Jordan wrenched the steering wheel, pulling the car over to the shoulder of the road. He killed the engine and the rain pattered heavily on the car roof, a cottony roaring that shut off the outside world.

"Kat . . ." He touched her hair and she jerked away, her eyes wide and tortured.

"What do you want?" she asked, her voice thick with tears. "What more can I give you?"

"Oh, kitten, don't look at me that way. It tears me up inside. I don't want to hurt you." A muscle in Jordan's jaw twitched.

"Then what do you want? I can't read you. I can't tell what you're feeling. Do *you* even know?"

He swallowed. "I'm afraid."

Kat's eyes widened at the raw truth in his husky confession. "Why?"

He draped both arms over the steering wheel and stared out at the rainy countryside. "I'm afraid that I'll start to care too much. Afraid that if I do, you'll disappear again."

"I won't," she whispered. "You can be sure of that. Give me a chance to prove it to you."

The car was quiet except for the rhythmic beat of the rain. Kat saw his jaw work, then he turned back to her. The warm toffee color of his eyes glinted with an inner coppery fire. His words were slow and precise, and as solemn as any courtroom decision.

"I'm not sure of anything anymore, except that after last night I can't give you up again."

A slow rush of color flamed Kat's cheeks. "You won't have to."

"I think we ought to back off for a while."

"You mean not see each other at all?"

"No, but . . . last night was a mistake."

"Oh, swell!" Kat threw up her hands in confusion and chagrin.

A reluctant chuckle escaped Jordan. His grin was crooked and he brushed a thumb over Kat's pink cheek in a brief caress. "No, not the way you think. That part of it was fantastic. But the timing was bad. You were upset. It was just too soon."

"Too soon?" she echoed, bewildered.

"I've had trouble realizing the changes eleven years have made. I took out my frustrations on you."

"Is that why you made love to me?" she asked in a low, tremulous voice. "Because you were frustrated?"

"That and a thousand other reasons, including that what you do to me is powerful chemistry, lady. But it tends to cloud the issue."

"What issue?"

"Whether you and I can have a relationship based on who we are now, not who we were."

"Is that what you want, Jordan? A relationship?" Her lips, pink and parted like rose petals, trembled with burgeoning hope.

He caught her hand and lifted her fingers to his lips. His words were low and ragged with emotion. "I don't think I can live with anything less."

"Jordan. Oh, Jordan!" Her features relaxed visibly with relief, and her smile was radiant, if a bit wobbly.

"Trust is a fragile thing, and mine was seriously shaken when you left, Kat. I'll admit I have a hard time separating that from what's here and now. We were just kids, and kids make mistakes. And you've been through a lot recently. Maybe you're just looking for an easy answer with me, anything to fill the void that quitting your job and losing a partner and friend left in your life."

"Oh, no, that's not true!"

He raised a hand to silence her protest. "I've got to be sure. No more mistakes."

"I love you, Jordan. I think I've shown you how much," she said in a low voice. She raised her head and her blue eyes glistened with moisture. "I don't know what else I can do to prove it to you."

His fingers tightened on hers. "Let's just give ourselves

144

some time," he said gently. His expression took on a teasing, boyish quality. "So what do you say? Can we agree to take a—a 'time out' physically and do some old-fashioned courting? If we can make it work between us on that basis, the rest will come naturally. How about it? Is it a deal?"

"Hmm. You mean, no more . . . uh, you know?"

"Uh-uh."

Relief and new hope made Kat suddenly aware of the humor in his suggestion. She decided she could do a little teasing too. "We can't even go parking out at the Battlepark to neck like we used to?"

"Nope."

Her eyes glinted. "What about an occasional good-night kiss?"

Jordan laughed. "That should be safe enough, I suppose. We'll take it slow and easy, get to be friends again. Deal?" He offered his hand.

Kat's lips twitched. Somehow she wasn't at all sure Jordan knew quite what he was getting himself into. The attraction between them had always been volatile. Did he really think this idea would work? But he seemed so earnest about it. And he was hinting at a real commitment. It was a small price to pay to give Jordan the time he needed to learn to trust her again. Happiness bubbled up within her like champagne, making her feel giddy and mischievous.

"Yes, it's a deal," she said. "But before we shake on it, could I do something first?"

"What?"

"This." She wrapped her arms around his neck and covered his mouth with hers. She felt his start of surprise, then his arms circled her back to pull her closer. She put her whole heart into it, conveying her love in a silent message.

I'm here. I'm yours. I love you.

She broke away, breathless and smiling. She took his

145

hand, but she felt no answering response or squeeze. Kat suppressed a laugh at his bemused state.

"Jordan? I'm ready now."

"Oh." He gave himself a tiny shake, focusing on her uplifted face. They shook hands solemnly, then slowly broke into smiles.

"You know what?" she said softly.

"What?"

"I think I'm ready for that hamburger now."

Jordan roared with laughter. "With onions, no doubt."

"Of course!" She gave him a mildly astounded look. "There's no need to worry about bad breath under our pact, is there?"

"None at all."

"Then make it two, with french fries and rings."

Jordan laughed and started the car. The rain was gone and the sun peeked out from behind a cloud.

"Uh, Jordan? One more question about this agreement." Kat batted her lashes in feigned innocence.

"What's that?" He knew her well enough to feel slightly suspicious.

"This is a modern arrangement, a real eighties relationship, isn't it?"

"Um, yeah, I guess so."

"So who pays for the hamburgers?"

"Golly, I could certainly get used to this kind of life!" Leann's short curls bounced around her plump face and she took another sip of her frozen piña colada. She leaned across the tiny table toward Kat and said in a conspiratorial whisper, "All this money floating around makes me sort of crazy."

Kat's laughter drifted above the muted rumble of the racing crowd at Bossier City's Louisiana Downs track. They sat in the upper level of boxes behind the plate glass wall overlooking the oval track. "Too bad none of it belongs to us."

"Yet! But if Don's hunches are correct, some of it will soon. I can hardly wait for the first race. How long does it take to place a bet, anyway?"

"Not long, but don't get your hopes up. Nobody ever got rich betting on the horses," Kat advised with a chuckle.

"You're cool enough now, but I'll bet you change your tune when Jordan's horse runs." Leann picked up the numbered racing form. "What's her name again?"

"Dream Tender. Sixth race. And you're right." Kat grinned. "I've got my two dollars ready to bet on one of Sabrina's foals. I'll be yelling my lungs out with the rest of them!"

"See there?" Leann giggled, looking at her friend with real fondness, admiring the cool, elegant figure Kat made in her slim halter dress and sophisticated chignon. "I can hardly believe Jordan was able to tear himself away from work long enough to come out here today, much less give you the day off. I know how devoted you are to those horses."

"He's been busy, but he wouldn't have missed Dream Tender's maiden race for anything. And it gave him a good excuse to try out the new man. If he works out at the farm, then Jordan's going to hire him full time in my place. I only wanted the job temporarily to tide me over."

Kat mentally crossed her fingers at the fib. She had connived and manipulated to get that job so she could be near Jordan. Thank God, it had worked.

"Do you ever miss your old job?" Leann asked curiously.

"It's funny you should ask. Don't tell Jordan, but I just got a letter from my former bureau chief asking if I'd go on special assignment with a news team he's forming."

"Are you thinking of accepting it?" Leann's voice was a bit alarmed.

Kat shook her head. "I'm not even tempted. Oh, there are some things I miss, but I like to think that's a chapter in my life that's over, and it's time to go on to other things. I want to get the photography business going. It's been too long since I held a camera. That's part of the reason I lugged all this gear up here today." She gestured to the equipment bag on the floor beside her chair.

"Well, you ought to get some interesting shots around this place," Leann remarked. Her eyebrows lifted exaggeratedly, and her eyes followed a Texan in boots and hat and diamond pinky ring with an overblown blonde on his arm. "By the way, your pictures of the girls are terrific. Their grandparents are thrilled with the ones I sent."

"I enjoyed working with them. I'd like to do more portrait work, especially with children. You are showing those proofs around, aren't you?" Kat nibbled delicately at the spear of pineapple from her drink.

"Sure thing!" Leann paused, an odd look on her face. She snapped her fingers. "I've just had a flash of inspiration, Kat. There's a charity fund-raising project my women's club was considering a while back. If you aren't looking to make a lot of money . . ."

"Just to cover expenses will be enough, if there's some chance to pick up business later."

"Then this would be perfect." Leann briefly outlined the project, which would involve Kat photographing children, then, for a donation, the pictures would be entered in a "healthy baby" picture contest. The winners would all be run in the local newspaper.

"It sounds like a wonderful opportunity," Kat said enthusiastically, and they agreed that Leann would set it up and supply Kat with details.

"I'm so glad that's settled," beamed Leann. "You know, Kat, I'm glad you and Jordan are back together. It's done you good. You look relaxed and happy."

"I am happy. We're getting along very well."

Kat smiled, and her inner serenity was reflected in her expression. She had to admit that things over the last month hadn't been easy at first, maybe because they had both been trying too hard. They'd had to carve time to be together out of their busy schedules. But somewhere along the line things had gotten easier, maybe because they were growing more familiar with each other, gradually relearning all there was to know about Kat and Jordan.

They had had fun cooking a spaghetti dinner at Jordan's one evening, then had to apologize profusely to Bertie for the mess they made. They talked over the phone late into the night, about nothing and everything. They talked horses and politics and books lazing side by side on the patio lounges beside Jordan's pool until hunger or the mosquitoes drove them in. They'd gone to the movies and sat through a double feature, sharing the giant tub of buttered popcorn, licking the salt from their greasy fingers and laughing together when Kat screamed at the scary parts of the horror movies.

And as each tentative revelation occurred, as the bonds of spiritual intimacy and genuine liking grew stronger with each passing day, Kat fell more deeply in love. And grew increasingly more frustrated.

All the warm feelings inside her longed to be expressed, but Jordan seemed determined to keep his word, to keep a physical distance between them that was never breached by more than a brotherly hug or a chaste brush of lips. Kat hoped that he was finding this self-imposed celibacy as hard as she was. But she did her best not to do anything that would torment either of them, respecting Jordan's self-control and the improvement in their relationship, if not exactly enjoying it.

She was always aware of Jordan, and sometimes just listening to him breathe was enough to twist her into knots. She tried to keep her thoughts away from the night they'd spent together, but often her fingers tingled with the repressed urge to touch him, to run her hands through his curling chest hair, exploring the hard ridges of muscle she knew lay beneath the sedate dress shirt and suit. Yes, she respected his wishes, and kept her part of the bargain, but she couldn't help wishing sometimes that he'd decide it was time to let nature take its course—and damn soon.

"It's probably none of my business," Leann said, self-consciously stirring her creamy drink with her straw, "but are there going to be wedding bells anytime soon?"

"It's too early to tell," Kat returned lightly. That was something that bothered her. Jordan had not started any discussion of plans for a future together. And, although she told him frequently that she loved him, he had never spoken those words to her. Kat did not think it was an oversight and told herself that when the time was right for Jordan, he'd say it. But it was hard not to be impatient.

"You ought to bring the subject up," Leann advised. "You know I proposed to Don, don't you?"

"Oh, Leann, I couldn't!" Kat said, laughing.

"You're going to have to do something soon. Jordan looks . . . looks . . ."

"Looks how?"

"Well, you remember Mrs. Thomas in ninth-grade English? In *Julius Caesar* when they talked about that 'lean and hungry look'? Well, that's how Jordan looks when he looks at you. Like he's starving to death for something."

Kat barely restrained her laughter. When Leann looked at her curiously, she tried to straighten her face, but her explanation was choked. "Let's just say that he's been on a diet."

"On a diet? Oh!" Leann's puzzled expression changed to understanding and she blushed, then dissolved into giggles. The women were still smiling into their palms and snickering when Don and Jordan came back from the betting window.

The talk revolved around daily doubles, exactas, the

Super Six, the favorites in each race and the long shots. Jordan stood behind Kat's chair chatting, his hand resting lightly on the curve of her bare shoulder. At one point he reached past her to pick up his drink, then dipped and placed an absentminded kiss on the side of her neck. Leann winked at Kat and giggled, then choked on her drink when Don demanded to know the joke.

The afternoon passed pleasantly. They bet for fun, two dollars at a time, winning some, losing some. But the tension was suddenly rife when the call came for the sixth race. They all went downstairs and outside to stand by the railing.

"Don't get your hopes up," Jordan warned. "This is Dream Tender's first outing, and the odds reflect it."

"I've got everything crossed but my eyes," Kat replied, holding her ticket like a talisman.

Jordan laughed and slung an arm around her waist to protect her from the crowd. The crush of people separated them from Don and Leann. The weight of his arm was solid and substantial against her back, and her Nikon on its strap bumped against her hip. Suddenly Kat wanted to tell him to forget the race, forget the crowd, and just hold her. It was all very fine to be calm and logical about things, but her heart wanted to run away from her and she longed for the passionate madness of his caresses, the magic spell of his kisses.

The starting bell brought her thoughts back to earth with a jolt and she yelled and cheered, urging the horse on. Somehow it seemed only right that Dream Tender won, and by half a length at that.

"She did it! By God, she did it!" Jordan shouted. Impulsively, he caught Kat close and kissed her. He regretted it immediately.

Damn! He'd been so careful to keep out of temptation's way, but her lips clung to his. He groaned, deepening the kiss intimately, tasting the faint residue of coconut and pineapple from her drink, ignoring the surging crowd around them. He pulled away at last and felt Kat shiver. Her lashes flickered, and when she opened her eyes he saw they were glazed with naked longing.

He swallowed harshly, his grin strained and a trifle crooked. Damn, he ached for her! He must have been out of his mind to dream up this crazy bargain of theirs. He'd taken more cold showers in the past month than he'd need in a lifetime! All because he'd wanted to have all the facts, to be sure. Of what, he wasn't certain any longer. But he'd made her a promise.

"Sorry."

"Who's complaining?" Kat smiled, then swiftly raised her camera and snapped a picture of his befuddled countenance. "Come on. I think you're wanted in the winner's circle—and I intend to record on film your moment of glory!"

Rosalind Scott stepped into her son's Adams Street law office looking like a lady just killing time as she was waved on through by the smiling secretary. One would have been hard pressed to guess that she was a woman with a mission.

"Jordan, dear! I hope I'm not interrupting anything?"

Jordan rose from his desk, abandoning for the moment the pile of mail he was reading. "Of course not, Mother. I always have time for you."

"Now, dear, you can't say that's been exactly true just recently."

Jordan seated her in a side chair and then rested lightly on the corner of his desk, crossing his arms.

"I've been very busy." His shrug was noncommittal.

"I understand you've been seeing a lot of Katherine Holt lately," Rosalind remarked.

"Your sources are correct as usual, Mother. You know, I'd be glad to answer any questions you have. You don't

152

have to keep tabs on me by dealing with the gossips at the beauty parlor."

"Jordan, really! I'm not trying to pry. It's just that a mother is always concerned about the welfare of her child. I hope you aren't getting too attached."

"I'm afraid I am. Very attached. Kat and I are . . . well, I just hope you'll get used to the idea."

"For as long as she stays in Mansfield?"

Jordan frowned. "What are you talking about? She's home to stay."

Rosalind examined the brass catch on her handbag. "Oh, dear. I hope I'm not speaking out of turn. It's just that I saw her outside the newspaper office just now talking to Paul Hartman. You know, he just got back from Washington. I can't help wondering if a young woman like Katherine doesn't miss the excitement and the glamour of her old job."

"Kat's too busy to think about it. She's making children's portraits at the *Enterprise* office today. Some sort of promotion for Leann's club."

"Nevertheless, once the wanderlust is in a person's blood . . . well, I'm sure Mansfield doesn't have much to offer, at least to Kat."

"It has me." Jordan's words were clipped, irritated.

"Will that be enough? It wasn't before," Rosalind pointed out with careful cruelty. She was rewarded when his jaw tightened.

Why did his mother have to strike right to the heart of his insecurity about Kat? Especially now when everything seemed to be going so well between them? He tried to squelch the feelings of unrest and doubt.

Rosalind continued, "Besides, what about Sondra?"

"What about Sondra? We certainly hadn't made any commitments. I heard she's been seeing Dennis Larsen recently, anyway. They were high-school sweethearts." He smiled suddenly. "So you see, Kat and I aren't the only ones finding romance with an old flame."

"An affair, you mean," Rosalind snapped, her features going cold.

Jordan straightened, scowling. "It might surprise you, but no, not exactly."

"I hate to see you wasting your time on that hussy!"

"I'm pretty well beyond needing your permission, Mother."

The intercom on his desk buzzed, then his secretary's voice announced the arrival of Ms. Holt. Jordan pressed a button. "Thank you, Marsha. Send her in." He released the button and his gaze returned to his mother. "That 'hussy' and I are having lunch together at the Old Church Inn, Mother. Would you care to join us?"

"No, thank you." Rosalind's lips thinned in frustration. She wouldn't have minded lunch at the charming Southern-style restaurant in the back of an old renovated church, but she was particular about the company she kept and refused to give tacit approval to this relationship by her presence. "I certainly hope that you don't regret getting involved with her again. It seems you haven't learned from past experience."

"I'll see you out." Jordan's voice was stiff. "I'd appreciate your being cordial to Kat. She's important to me."

"I was brought up a lady, Jordan. You needn't lecture me on good breeding!"

"It's so hot!" Kat complained with a sigh. She drained the last of the iced tea from her frosty glass.

"Then go swimming." Jordan's voice was muffled. He lay on his stomach on the lounge beside the glittering blue water of the swimming pool at the rear of his house.

"It's so boring." Seated in the lounge next to him, Kat let her gaze travel down the long, muscular length of his legs. As the sun dried the moisture from his tanned skin, the soft hairs began to curl again.

"Then don't go swimming."

"But it's hot!"

Jordan raised his head and squinted against the afternoon sun, then gave her a disgusted look. Grumbling under his breath he buried his face in his arms again.

"I have an idea," she said brightly. "Let's go down to the old swimming hole."

"Uh-uh. Too tired."

"Jordan, please," she cajoled. She stretched her leg and ran her big toe down his calf. He jerked away.

"Cut it out, Kat."

This whole setup was making her bitchy, Kat reflected irritably.

She lay back in a mock sulk. "Well, if you wouldn't swim so many laps, you wouldn't be in this condition!"

But it was the only thing keeping him sane, Jordan thought. The tight grimace he made stayed hidden against his arms.

Not one to take no for an answer, Kat swung her legs around and sat up, tugging down the bottom of her maillot bathing suit. Thoughtfully, she studied Jordan's spine and the cold glass in her hand. Deliberately, she set the icy glass on his hot skin.

"Yeow! What the hell?" Jordan jackknifed up, catching a laughing Kat before she could dance away. "Are you crazy, woman? You could give a man a heart attack like that!"

Crazy about him, Kat thought, sublimely conscious of his warm skin pressed against hers. Her laughter died away.

A heart attack would be a merciful release, Jordan groaned inwardly, fighting the stirring of desire low in his body.

Kat's mouth was suddenly dry, her breath erratic. She

stared up into his eyes, her hands on his bare, sun-warmed shoulders. Was it up to her to make the first move? But before she could decide, Jordan was firmly setting her away.

"Maybe we'd better check the swimming hole out at that," he muttered hoarsely. Kat tried to keep the disappointment out of her face and mutely gathered up towels and sandals. She jerked on her shirt, a gift from Jordan, a yellow T with the words "Have You Hugged Your Thoroughbred Today?" emblazoned on the front. It occurred to her that lately the horses had been more affectionate than this stubborn, mule-headed man! She vowed that the next opportunity she had to move along her relationship with Jordan would not be wasted. Curiously, Jordan was thinking along the same lines.

The trek through the woods was curiously silent, each keeping his own counsel. They reached the glen and headed for the sandy shore, past the distorted L-shaped tree. The sun dappled the still water, sparkling over it in shining patterns of light and shadow. Kat and Jordan stood side by side, silently looking at the pool, each remembering. Kat's quiet words broke the hush.

"Jordan? I have a confession to make."

"Oh?"

Her heart thumped mightily in her chest as she gathered up her courage. "I didn't come out here to go swimming."

"Neither did I," he replied softly.

In the next instant they were in each other's arms, the forced restraint of the past weeks shattering in a passionate explosion. Starved mouths sought, held. Hungry hands caressed, fluttered, clung. Jordan lifted his head, his breath puffing against her flushed cheeks.

"Who the hell thought of this stupid arrangement, anyway? It was a bad idea." His smile cocked at an angle and his hands slid down her back to pull her even closer.

"A very bad idea," Kat agreed, pressing against him

ardently. Her shaky laugh faltered at the golden blaze of desire in his warm brown eyes.

Gently, slowly, Jordan pulled her down on the soft grass. "Let's see if we can think of something better."

CHAPTER TEN

"This is much better."

Kat's breath was a wispy sigh against Jordan's hungry mouth. Side by side, they lay in the lush grasses at the water's edge, arms wrapped about each other as if they would never let go again.

"It's not as good as it's going to get," Jordan murmured. His hand slid down over the rounded curve of her buttock, pulling her closer. Her breath rushed into her lungs as the throbbing proof of his desire pressed against her thigh.

"Promises, promises," she teased in a husky voice. Her hands moved restlessly over his bare shoulders, kneading his hard muscles, stroking the taut cords of his neck. She dipped her head and blew softly into the nest of dark curls at the base of his throat, then inhaled the essence of his skin, totally arousing, uniquely Jordan.

Jordan's fingers twined into the thick mass of her fair hair, gently tilting her face up to his. He saw the glazed look in her eyes and knew that she wanted him. The knowledge of her desire fed his need, stoked the heat in his loins. With a groan, he took her mouth again.

His tongue outlined her lips with a wet, sensuous sweep, circling again and again until she moaned helplessly. Only then did he take full possession of her mouth, seeking out all the moist, secret places, tracing the line of her perfect teeth, plunging deeply. He wanted to devour her until she was a part of him. The last time they were together she had come to him in the fullness of her sorrow. He couldn't rid himself of the sneaking uncertainty that only that need had brought her to him. This time he would somehow make her his, make her dependent on him, bind her to him for eternity, and make her realize that only he could fill her need.

He released her mouth, nibbled down her throat while he tugged at the hem of her shirt, pulling it over her head and flinging it aside.

"My, the liberties you do take, sir!" Kat gasped, her words slurred with the come-hither drawl of a Southern belle.

"You have on too many damn clothes," he complained. The tight bathing suit frustrated his attempts to touch her everywhere.

Kat laughed, a low, seductive sound that stirred his hunger. Since the outcome of this encounter was a foregone conclusion, she could afford to savor the moment by teasing him. Perhaps even repay him in small part for the past weeks of frustration.

"I think we'd better stop."

"What?" His hands stilled on the elastic strap of the suit. He instantly relaxed when he saw her sultry, provocative smile.

"I'm not at all convinced our agreement covers what you're trying to do to me. Does this kind of thing happen between *friends?*"

Jordan grinned, then pulled the swimsuit strap past her elbow, releasing one full breast to his heated gaze. His palm covered the rounded mound and his thumb rubbed the sensitive tip. "This is what's known as doing what comes naturally."

"But do we really know each other well enough?" Kat gasped. Jordan peeled away the other strap.

"If we don't, we're about to." His mouth dipped to suckle ardently on the turgid nipple of the other breast.

159

Kat arched against him, urging him to take more of the rosy crest into his mouth. Her teasing words wavered.

"But . . ."

"Shut up, woman," Jordan mumbled, "and let me love you."

Kat did so gladly.

He urged her gently to her back, pushing her down into the soft grass, slowly rolling the elastic fabric of her suit down inch by inch. To each bit of skin newly revealed, he paid his homage, caressing it with his fingers, saluting it with his lips. Kat's breath caught in her throat at the agonizing snail's pace of his ministrations, but he would not be rushed. His fingers tangled in the tawny curls at the juncture of her thighs, then swept the offending suit down her legs and away.

Kat writhed in excitement, her breath coming in raspy, erratic gasps. Her fingers threaded through the burnished strands of his hair and she crooned her need for him with soft, breathless love words. She pulled him to her, and he found her lips again, tugging at the swollen underlip with the edge of his teeth.

The odor of crushed grass rose around them; the sun warmed and dappled their sweat-soaked bodies. Kat moved her hand under the waistband of Jordan's swim trunks, felt the resulting tremor wrack him.

"You have on too many damn clothes," she murmured against his lips. Her fingers eagerly worked the garment away from him. Jordan gave a moment's assistance, then covered her fully with his lean body, and Kat sighed with the welcome pressure of his weight.

The civilized restrictions of clothing discarded completely, their lovemaking changed into something wild and primitive there among the forest clearing. His fingers sought, parted her warm female petals, dipped and stroked. She was wet and ready for him. Her hand surrounded his shaft, caressed the velvety length, the sensitive tip. Steel encased in silk, warm and alive in her palm.

Jordan drew back, looked down into Kat's passion-glazed face and felt as new as Adam. And she was all Eve, womanly, curved, made just to fit a man. She raised her arms to call him home and Jordan felt the heat of his manhood surge near to bursting.

With a sudden lunge, he caught her to him, rolled her above him. Just as wildly, Kat positioned her hips, then took him all within herself. He slid into the wet, glistening confines of her flesh and groaned. She gasped in answer, her hands pushing against his chest. He held her hips firmly, guiding her upward, then down, increasing the rhythm into a pounding crescendo.

Suddenly, shudders of overwhelming pleasure shook her and she rode the waves of fulfillment to an inner shore, collapsing onto his chest. Her inner contractions triggered his release. His arms tightened about her for the deep final thrust to completion. He groaned her name, rhythmic spasms culminating in splendor as he followed her to that secret place.

Chests heaving, they lay together, spent, satiated, utterly content.

"I have the feeling this may be the beginning of a beautiful friendship," Kat drawled at last.

Laughter started low in Jordan's throat, then rang out in joyous abandon to mingle with the twitters of birds under the green forest roof. His arms circled her, rocking her back and forth. For the moment all doubts, all apprehensions were suspended and he merely enjoyed the rightness of her in his arms.

"God! How good you feel," he muttered, smiling into her hair.

"Mmm. I feel rather—exposed." She laughed, rolling from him with a gusty sigh. "Not to mention that the insect

161

population seems to be taking dinner reservations on my hide!"

"Complaints so soon?" He broke off a grass stem and languidly chewed on its end. His eyes raked her love-dampened body. "You used to be made of tougher stuff. Brings back memories, doesn't it?" He trailed the seed-heavy grass pod across her breasts and she shivered.

"They were very sweet, those first times here with you." She grinned and sat up gingerly, splendid in her unselfconscious nudity. "Not that I've got anything against a good old-fashioned mattress!"

"Poor baby." He rolled lithely to his feet and scooped her up, an arm behind her knees and shoulders. "What you have to put up with!"

"Jordan! What are you doing?" She laughed.

He waded out into the pool. "I recall we did a fair amount of skinny-dipping."

"Rusty, no! You rat! Oh!" She kicked and squealed when the tepid water lapped at her bare bottom. Ignoring her cries, Jordan plunged in. Kat came up spluttering, pushing her streaming hair out of her eyes. "You . . . you . . ."

Her words faltered when his large hands pulled her close. His mouth closed over hers in a dizzying kiss, then moved to sip the water dripping from her breasts. Desire ignited again and she whimpered. Kat clutched his head, tracing the curves of his ears with her fingers, and their legs brushed sensuously under the liquid covers of the pool.

"Come to me, kitten," Jordan whispered hoarsely. "Show me the memories haven't died." Boldly, he surged upward, making her gasp with the rampant proof of his desire. Eagerly, gladly, Kat answered him and gave herself up to the marvel of his embrace.

"You're going to be late for work."

"Yup."

Kat paused in her puttering with the breakfast things and smiled at Jordan. He stood in the open doorway of her kitchen, clad only in a towel hitched about his lean hips. He rubbed his damp hair with another towel and eyed Kat appreciatively, a slow, slumberous smile on his lips.

"You don't care?" she asked.

"Not at the moment." His glance flicked to the clock on the stove. "There's plenty of time before I have to drive to Baton Rouge."

"This trip came up rather suddenly, didn't it?"

His expression clouded over for a moment, then he shrugged. "My business won't take me long. I'll be back tomorrow evening."

"I'll miss you."

"I'll hurry home." He sat down in the chrome kitchen chair, admiring the tantalizing glimpses of her through the thin, silky robe she wore. He draped the towel about his neck, feeling the renewed stirrings of desire. "Come here, woman."

Laughing softly, Kat padded over on bare feet to stand between his outstretched legs. She laced her fingers into the damp, springly curls at his nape and kissed him lightly. He smelled of soap and shaving cream and warm male skin. "Good morning."

"Absolutely." His fingers tightened on her waist and he nudged the wrapped front of her robe aside with his nose, nuzzling her breasts with his lips.

Kat caught a ragged breath. His tongue flicked out, doing delightful things to her skin. Her laugh was shaky. "You're insatiable, Jordan."

"Honey, a starvation diet will do it to you." He pulled back and grinned up at her. "I was late getting to the banquet and I've got to make up for lost time, haven't I?"

"Gluttony is a sin," she teased.

"So is lust," he shot back.

"Then I guess we'll both go to hell." She sighed.

"It feels like paradise to me." He nipped at her mouth, tugged at her bottom lip with his teeth.

Kat shivered under his sensual onslaught. "I repeat, sir. You are insatiable."

"We were rather unrestrained yesterday at the swimming hole, weren't we?"

"Unrestrained?" She laughed. "I think I've still got grass stains on my buns!"

"That's too bad." His hands slid under the hem of her robe to caress that silky-skinned portion of her anatomy. "If you decide to wash them off I know a volunteer who'd like to help."

Kat laughed and playfully slapped at his groping hands. "Unhand me, you varmint! Breakfast is almost ready."

"I've worked up an appetite of a different nature."

"But . . ." Her protests were cut short by Jordan's mouth on hers. Strong arms pulled her down so that she rested fully against him as he leaned back in the chair. She squirmed sinuously, relishing the tactile pleasures of damp, hairy male skin against cool, smooth silk and female flesh.

Their coming together beside the swimming hole had been wild, explosive. The uninhibited exploration of the wonderful differences between male and female led them eventually to Kat's house, to the comfort of Kat's old-fashioned mattress. Leisurely, almost agonizingly slow lovemaking filled with mutual tenderness consumed the night until the final flare of excitement exploded in a blazing finale. Kat was amazed at the need they found for each other, the infinite variety and endless range of sensations evoked by Jordan's lovemaking. She knew she would never tire of him. Sweet words, sensual caresses—they couldn't get enough of each other.

Each time was different, new, Jordan thought, his mind drugged with the heady deliciousness of Kat's mouth, the intoxication of her presence. She responded selflessly, always giving, always loving. How he loved this woman.

The realization came almost as a feeling of relief, a letting go of old pain so that joy could be found in the present moment. This was where he always wanted to be, close to her. This was where he belonged. Only with Kat was he a whole man.

He lifted his lips from hers, catching her chin with his fingers and smiling down into her face with aching tenderness in his expression. Her breathing fluttered and her gaze met his, soft and yielding.

"My darling Kat." The words seemed to clog in his throat with emotion too thick to express.

"Breakfast can wait," Kat whispered.

"I'm hungry only for you."

Their lips met again. The sharp, jarring peal of the telephone startled them. They groaned simultaneously.

"Damn. I'll get it," Kat said, sliding reluctantly off of Jordan. She raked a trembling hand through her hair and smiled.

"Hurry back." His languorous expression held a wealth of promise.

He heard the soft murmur of her voice from the front room. Rising, he poured a mug of black coffee from the battered tin pot on the stove. Was this what living with Kat would be like? The easy companionship spiced with early-morning loving? It was easy to picture her in his home, always there, warming his hearth with her presence, his heart with her smile, and his bed . . . Ah, well, there indeed was good cause for a man to think about settling down with the right woman. And it was increasingly clear that Kat was the right woman—the only woman—for Jordan Scott. Smiling slightly to himself, he took a sip of the coffee and ambled after her.

"It sounds too good to be true, Mort." She stood beside the desk, a small frown between her brows. She tugged the overlong phone cord out of the way, then rubbed the pleat on her forehead and stared unseeingly into space. "London, you said? Then Berlin, Geneva . . . Yes, I understand."

Jordan stopped short, slapped out of a warm, delightful reverie by an icy hand. Chilling dread clutched at his gut and his knuckles went white on the handle of the mug. Rosalind's warnings returned to mock him. Dreams dissolved into ashes and a burning rage tore through him as he saw history repeating itself.

"How much?" Kat's tone was incredulous, and she paused and listened again to the voice on the other end of the wire. "Well, I'm extremely flattered, but . . . yes, I suppose I could think about it . . . yes, yes, all right. Good-bye, Mort."

She hung up the phone slowly, her expression thoughtful, a tiny, pleased smile on her lips.

"I suppose that's what you've been waiting for," Jordan bit out. Anger and betrayal serrated his words. "Your ticket out of here!"

Kat whirled around, startled by the harshness of his voice. "What are you talking about?"

"Don't play innocent with me," he yelled. "God! Just when I thought . . . Okay, fine! Take off! It's what you've wanted all along, isn't it?"

"Jordan! That's not true!" Kat's face mirrored shock and amazement at this sudden attack.

"Don't lie to me, Katherine! I heard it all!"

"Evidently not!" she snapped. "Or you'd have heard me turn down Mort's offer!"

"Sure, you think you can turn it down now, but I saw the light in your eyes. How long will it take before you change your mind? A week, another month, maybe?" He knew vaguely that he was being unreasonable, but fear

166

held him in its icy grip. He was losing her again! His only defense against the shattering pain, the promise of screaming loneliness was to attack.

"This is crazy!" Kat cried. "I'm not leaving. I told Mort I wasn't interested. I'm not going anywhere!"

"What kind of guarantee do you care to make? Until you tire of me, or until you get a better offer? Aw, hell!" He slammed the mug down on a table, slopping the coffee over its rim, and turned away. "I knew nothing would hold you for long!"

"Jordan, please." Kat, bewildered and feeling increasingly desperate, ran after him. "What's the matter with you? You've got to listen!"

He turned on her, catching her shoulders in a fierce grip. "Listen to what? More lies?"

"I never lied to you!" Her face flushed under his intense scrutiny. "At least," she faltered, remembering the one giant lie from long ago. "At least, not about loving you, and not now, about wanting to be with you forever."

"You expect me to believe that?" His laugh grated harshly in her ears.

Her lip trembled and a single tear washed down her cheek. "What can I say? What do I have to do? I love you, and somewhere along the line you have to accept that on faith and trust me. Do I have to keep proving myself over and over?"

"Yes!"

Her shoulders slumped in dejection beneath his hands. "I don't know what else to try. Even a criminal is presumed innocent, but I'm guilty no matter what I do."

"You condemned yourself a long time ago," he said.

"And you're going to make me pay and pay, is that it?" Anger compressed her lips and she shook off his hands in repressed fury. "Judge, jury, and executioner all rolled into one. You can't make love in a courtroom, Jordan!"

"It never occurred to me that you could."

167

"You never forgive and never forget. You're always holding something back." A terrible understanding surged into her turbulent thoughts. "Maybe you don't want to believe in me," she said slowly.

"You're not making sense!"

"Hating me gives you the excuse you need, so you never have to risk anything of yourself. There's a larger problem here than whether I go or stay. It's whether you can trust me to love you no matter what. But you can't trust until you're willing to commit everything you have, Jordan, your heart and soul. I understand now why you always believe the worst of me—you can blame me if things go sour."

"I can't stand here listening to you babble, Katherine. I've got to go."

"That's right! Run!" she shouted. "Run so you won't hear the truth about yourself!"

Jordan's jaw tightened and his brow lowered ominously. Without another word he strode from the room, returning minutes later, half-dressed, his other clothes in a bundle under his arm. Kat stood against the kitchen doorframe, her arms crossed, holding herself in tight control. A sudden, yawning emotional gulf had opened between them, all the more tormenting for the sweetness and communication they had shared only a short time before.

He paused, his hand on the front door knob. Eyes collided across the room, across the gaping chasm that separated them. "We'll talk when I get back," he rumbled. *"If you're still here."*

A heavy weight pressed down on Kat's heart, his unrelenting lack of faith tearing at her with piercing talons. She swallowed back tears and her words were forlorn, utterly discouraged. "I'm not sure talk will help, but I'll be here."

168

CHAPTER ELEVEN

A breathing space. That's what they both needed, Kat decided. Emotional highs and lows were too draining. A person couldn't think coherently under so much strain.

She looked again at her wristwatch, then tossed aside the negatives on which she'd been pretending to work. The lower the sun sank, the farther her mind wandered.

Where was Jordan? Had he gotten home from Baton Rouge yet? Why hadn't he called? *Would* he call?

Kat sighed again and rubbed her tense neck. She felt as churned up inside as a psychotic blender! Why did loving Jordan have to be so difficult? She couldn't take much more of his on-again, off-again treatment. For a man who prided himself on his logic and good sense he was being very unreasonable. There had to be some way to settle this latest misunderstanding without resorting to her landing a two-by-four right between his stubborn brown eyes!

Kat's normal determination began to reassert itself. She hadn't come this far with Jordan to sit back and let their relationship slip right through her fingers. It was time to do some plain talking, to get things aired out once and for all. And, dammit, to demand whether or not his intentions were honorable.

Kat's mouth firmed into a stubborn line. And there was no time like the present. She grabbed her keys and headed for her car. If Jordan wasn't home then she'd wait. One way or the other it was time to settle the questions that threatened to keep them apart.

Kat was disappointed when she drove up the driveway to the farm. There was no sign of Jordan's car. Resolutely, she searched through the flowerpots at the back door, found Bertie's key, and let herself in. Kat prowled restlessly around the house, turning on a lamp here, straightening a cushion there. What was taking him so long?

She poured herself a glass of wine from the cabinet in the den and threw herself down in a chair. She flipped desultorily through a technical law publication, sipping the wine in the vain hope of soothing her ragged nerves. Moments later, she got up and began to pace. She perused the book-lined shelves, flicked on the television only to turn it off again, then wandered aimlessly around the room. Outside, the sun had disappeared. Tension coiled low in her stomach like a venomous serpent. The wall holding Jordan's awards caught her attention briefly, but her thoughts were chaotic and she stared unseeingly at the assorted trophies, fighting down the choking anxiety. She couldn't lose Jordan now. She couldn't!

"I see that you've been making yourself at home."

The acidic remark brought Kat out of her reverie like an ice-cold drenching. She whirled to face Rosalind Scott. "Mrs. Scott. I didn't hear you."

"Obviously." Rosalind set down her handbag, and her manicured nails clicked against the tabletop. "Daydreaming, I suppose. Probably rearranging the furniture. But then you were always one to covet Jordan's things—his home, his family, his situation in life."

So the white gloves were off, Kat thought wryly. Automatically, her spine stiffened, but her reply was quiet. "Jordan himself is the only thing I've ever coveted."

Rosalind eyed her narrowly. "Perhaps it's just as well that I found you before Jordan returns with his news. I've been wanting to talk to you."

Kat stared, an uneasy feeling of déjà vu seeping through her veins. She gave herself a shake. She was no longer a helpless seventeen-year-old.

"I don't think you have anything to say that would interest me," she said coldly.

"Not even the fact that Jordan is regretting his entanglement with you? And wondering how to bring it to an end gracefully? Men are never adroit at these things. It's up to us women to behave in a dignified manner."

Kat hesitated. Was there a grain of truth in what Rosalind said? Would that explain Jordan's recent behavior? Or was this just another example of Rosalind's ruthlessness? She suppressed the panic Rosalind's words had given rise to.

"My relationship with your son is not open for discussion. Even if what you insinuate is true, I seriously doubt Jordan would send you as an emissary. He is many things, but a coward is not one of them."

Rosalind gave a long-suffering sigh and sat primly on the edge of the sofa. "I had so hoped you would be reasonable," she complained. "It makes things so much more civilized, wouldn't you say?"

Kat shrugged. "I've seen enough of diplomacy and counter-diplomacy to know that so-called civilized people can be vicious and amoral under that façade of reason. So please, Mrs. Scott, will you just say what you have to say?"

Rosalind's face went livid under her perfectly applied makeup. "I think you should go back to wherever you came from and get out of Jordan's life!"

"That's hardly an original suggestion," Kat remarked, her voice deceptively mild and tinged with irony. "Suppose you give me one good reason."

"The most important one is that the next senator from Louisiana will need a wife he can be proud of."

"What?"

Rosalind's expression mirrored her trimph. "Ah, so he

171

hadn't told you! That in itself should be significant, even to one of your shallow understanding."

"I don't know what you mean."

"Where do you think he's been? This trip to Baton Rouge was the culmination of many years' work on my part, keeping the political lines open, keeping the Scott name alive until the time was right. Jordan has been offered the party's nomination. He'll win easily with my guidance and follow in the Scott political tradition. The last thing he needs at this point is the wrong kind of wife to drag him down!"

"He never said . . ." Kat's thoughts whirled in confusion.

"Exactly, my dear." Rosalind's voice oozed commiseration. "As painful as it may be, if you care at all for Jordan, it's imperative that you step aside immediately. From now on his career must come first."

"His career? Who decided that?" Kat demanded suddenly.

Rosalind looked a bit flustered. "Well, of course, you can see it's the only—"

"No, I can't see anything but the fact that you've forgotten the most important element of this twisted scenario— Jordan's happiness. And I can make him happy whatever his aspirations."

"A sordid kind of happiness that's doomed to fail in the end," Rosalind returned. "What Andrew and I wanted for Jordan was more solid, the fulfillment that comes from serving his country with the right sort of helpmate at his side."

"What did you and the senator ever do to make Jordan happy?" Kat demanded, her voice rising. Her eyes flashed and her tone became scathing. "When did you give him what he needed most? Two parents. A few moments of undivided attention. The only time he was ever off his best behavior was here at the farm. You stifled him! You're still

172

trying to. I think I know why Jordan first loved me, Mrs. Scott. Because I made him feel *free.*"

"Don't you dare talk about the senator in that manner!" Rosalind snapped, jumping to her feet.

Kat's laugh was bitter, resentful. "Oh, no, we mustn't sully the senator's name in any way! No matter that he wasn't as lily white as we like to believe!"

"He was acquitted," Rosalind said stiffly.

"Of course he was! What jury would convict the illustrious Senator Andrew Scott? Don't you think Papa John knew what the chances would be? It hurt him to have to go after a man he'd once supported and called friend. But his duty was to the public, just as was the senator's. Only your husband fumbled the ball. Oh, nothing so very bad. Not a felony, only a little venal back-slapping and under-the-table campaign contributions!"

Kat laughed again at Rosalind's stricken expression. "Did you think I didn't know? I saw the evidence Papa John turned over to the Grand Jury. I may have been young, but I wasn't stupid!"

"You—you never told Jordan?" Rosalind's voice was breathless, thready.

"What good would that have done?" Her voice was low, choked. "Oh, it was a fine choice you had me make! Break up with Jordan or you'd kill Papa John with a libel suit. The worst injustice was not what you did to me, but what you did to your own son. You took away his ability to trust. But I love him, and sooner or later he'll admit that he still loves me. So don't try to use any more scare tactics on me, Mrs. Scott. This time no one but Jordan will send me away!"

"I don't think that will be necessary, Kat." Jordan's tired, furious voice jerked the two women around, dismay written on both faces. He stood in the doorway, his features as harsh and bleak as an Arctic night.

Rosalind's brittle laugh broke the stunned silence. "Jordan! I didn't hear you drive up! How was your trip?"

"Spare me the pleasantries, Mother." He tossed his briefcase aside and pulled viciously at his tie. "Things are beyond that point."

Rosalind paled. "How long . . ."

"Long enough."

Kat watched him walk to the liquor cabinet and her emotions roiled like storm clouds. She was aghast at the revelations he'd overheard, hurting for him at the pain she saw in his eyes, and at the same time strangely relieved that at last everything was out in the open. He poured something amber and potent, tossed half of it to the back of his throat and swallowed harshly.

Jordan let the liquor burn down his throat, his senses reeling. All the stable, familiar landmarks of his life had crumbled before his very eyes, all because of the destructive power of a few short sentences. He glanced at Kat for the first time and his eyes blazed.

"So many things are finally clear to me. I can guess the rest."

Kat sank slowly to the edge of a chair, her knees shaky. She tugged unconsciously at her earring, her eyes wide with apprehension. He was in a high rage, but against whom—his mother, her, himself—she wasn't certain.

"It seemed the only way," Rosalind mumbled. She dug into her pocket and dabbed her eyes with a lace-trimmed handkerchief.

"So you threatened to sue John Holt unless Kat did as you said."

"You were too young to marry. Much too young."

"I only have one question. Did Dad know about this?"

Rosalind's lips trembled and she shook her head. "No, I never told Andrew what I'd done. I almost wish I had now. Maybe he could have stopped me before . . . before . . . Oh, Jordan, please try to understand," she cried. "I was only thinking of you! There was your education to consider —and your career."

Jordan's face darkened with fury. "So it all comes back to that? My damn career?"

"Yes! Oh, Jordan, you'll be the best senator this state has ever had!" exclaimed his mother.

"Not bloody likely. I turned them down." His voice was flat.

Rosalind gasped. "Oh, no!"

"Jordan, why?" Kat asked.

"It was never my ambition to follow in Dad's footsteps. It was always *your* ambition, Mother. I had enough of campaigning and politics growing up. I won't live my life just to fulfill yours." His expression was black with the turbulence of his emotions. Kat winced with Rosalind at his unrelenting words.

Rosalind's face collapsed as she saw her dreams die. She looked suddenly old, shriveled, and frail. "Then there's no more to say, is there?"

"No." Jordan stared down into his glass.

Amazingly, Kat pitied Rosalind, seeing her shattered look as she gazed at her only son's stony expression. Kat moved hesitantly to Jordan's side.

"Don't be so hard on her," she said. Rosalind looked up in astonishment at Kat's unexpected defense.

Jordan bit off an expletive. "How can you, of all people, say that?"

Kat shrugged. "She's not my mother."

"That's what makes it so damned sickening." He sank down on a chair, cradling the glass between his hands. He twirled the liquid around, then made a sound of disgust and set it aside. Anger, remorse, and guilt churned in his gut. "Why didn't you come to me? Why did you let her do it to us, Kat?"

"I didn't know what to do!" Kat drew a shaky breath, remembering. "I was so afraid, so powerless."

"But a libel suit? Do you realize how difficult that is to win in court?"

"I didn't then!" She forced calm into her tone. "Afterward, the damage was done and Papa John was gone."

"So you took the easy way out."

Her jaw went slack with amazement. "What?"

"It was easier to give in, easier to run than to have faith in me."

"Don't you try to turn this thing around on me! I was backed into a corner. I died a little each day knowing what I'd done to you. But you know what's really ironic? Fool that I was, I prayed that you'd come to me, that somehow you'd see through the lie."

Rosalind shifted uncomfortably.

Jordan stood up, his face a mask of misery. His fists clenched. "All I can see is betrayal on every side," he muttered.

His agony touched Kat. She sighed and her angry features eased as she laid a hand on his forearm. "It was a long time ago, Jordan. It won't do any good to hold it against me or your mother now. She's always had a blind spot where you're concerned, a sort of tunnel vision. I just got in the way."

"You're quite understanding, Katherine," Rosalind gulped. She mopped her cheeks and made a visible effort to pull herself together.

Jordan grabbed Kat's wrist in a painful grip. "Quite the cozy conspiracy," he sneered. "You never intended to tell me the truth, did you?"

"No." Kat shook her head.

"Why?"

"I knew it would hurt you."

"You did it all for my own good? Should I thank you for that?" he asked, his voice bitter. "You're no better than *she* is!"

Rosalind jerked at the icy contempt in her son's voice.

176

Kat paled, but her anger rose anew. She wrenched her wrist free and turned away, rubbing the bruised place. Her voice shook.

"If you can't see the difference, then there's no hope for us." Her eyes were almost feverishly bright as she brushed past Rosalind. "Congratulations, Mrs. Scott. It seems you've won—again."

"No, don't go!" Rosalind jumped to her feet in agitation. She nodded toward her glowering son. "Talk to him, please! I've done enough damage." With a surprising squeeze of Kat's hand, she scurried from the room and out the back door.

Kat slowly turned back to Jordan. He rubbed the back of his hand against his jaw in a gesture of indecision. His eyebrows lifted sardonically.

"Well, Katherine? Where do we go from here? I sure as hell don't know!"

Her expression softened and her eyes became a deep blue. "Oh, Jordan, can't you see? We're so lucky to get another chance together." She lifted one hand in tender appeal. "Can't we put all of this behind us once and for all? You have to believe in me now that you know the truth."

"I don't really have a choice, do I?" he asked roughly.

Kat stared at him, a terrible sinking feeling chilling her bones. Her hand fell away. She answered slowly, her voice trembling. "No, that's not true. There are always choices. You can choose to forgive me and your mother or not. You can choose to love me or not. You can choose to trust your heart or not."

"What do you want me to say? That I don't hold you responsible? There, I've said it. What more do you want?"

"Oh, Rusty." Her words were barely audible. Scalding tears squeezed from beneath her lids. "If you have to ask then you'll never know."

Kat looked up into Jordan's handsome, haggard face and

despaired. She couldn't reach him. Maybe she'd never be able to. So what choice did she have? Stay with him, accepting the few crumbs of himself he was willing to share? Live with his doubt and hope someday that he'd love her fully? Or go away again to preserve what was left of her sanity and individuality, and by leaving condemn herself in his eyes for all time?

A sob ripped from her throat as she saw her dreams shatter, her world collapse around her in brittle piercing shards. Frowning, Jordan took a step toward her, but she backed away.

"Kat? I don't understand."

She wiped her damp cheeks with fingers that shook. "You never have. And you won't now. I can't stand it any longer, Jordan. I can't wait until you're able to love me without qualifications."

There was a curious, blank look in Jordan's eyes. "You're leaving?"

"It's not about leaving or staying. It's about your ability to trust me and our love."

"But you're still leaving." His expression gave nothing away.

"You take everything, but you give nothing back. You warned me what you had to offer might not be enough. You were right. It's not."

"Why am I not surprised?" His voice and face were both hard.

Kat sighed, resigned. "I know you've been expecting something like this all along." Her face cracked in a grim caricature of a smile. "I didn't want to disappoint you."

At the door, she paused. The silence stretched between them, as arid and distant as an endless desert. Kat filled her eyes with him one last time as hope drained away. He would make no move to stop her, she knew.

"I've never stopped loving you, Jordan. I never will. When you figure it out, I'll be waiting."

CHAPTER TWELVE

The telephone began to ring just as Kat pushed her key into the cranky lock. She struggled under the weight of her loaded camera bags and duffel and finally kicked the door open, half falling into the apartment. She dropped her things on the faded linoleum and dashed for the jangling phone.

" 'Lo?" She was breathless. She tugged at the knitted wool cap that half covered her face. Outside, an unseasonable cold spell turned the night into a howling, whistling banshee, banishing all signs of the mild Washington October. "Oh, hello, Mort."

Holding the receiver between her ear and shoulder, Kat flipped on the light switch and picked up the pile of mail at her feet, grimacing in distaste at the dismal two-room apartment. She'd been lucky to find it, a sublet of a sublet, in crowded Arlington, but it was just as well Mort had kept her too busy since her return to the news bureau to be there much. She listened to her boss now in growing dismay.

"But Mort!" she wailed. "I'm just in from Rome! I haven't even read my mail yet! I know I asked for all the work you could give me, but this is ridiculous. Have a heart, will you?"

Mort's Brooklyn accent twanged in her ear. "Look, kid,

if there was any other way, I'd find it. But you dealt with Prime Minister Jubayl when you were in Lebanon."

She hesitated. "Yes, he . . . the bomb that killed Bill was intended for him. He sent his personal condolences." At least she could talk about it now, she thought to herself. Jordan healed her that much.

"All I want is for you to follow him around during his U.S. junket. We've got rumors that a compromise settlement between the major factions is in the works. I'll send Tony Scanlan with you."

"Tony? He's still wet behind the ears!"

Mort's laughter cackled. "That's what they used to say about you. Four-five days, tops. Then you get a couple of days off, okay?"

"You're a real pal, Mort."

"I knew you'd see it my way. Bright and early, okay?"

"Right."

Kat hung up the phone with a philosophical shrug. It was the nature of her work to have to go where the news was. She had plunged right back into the pressure cooker for lack of anything better to do with her life. After all, work was all she had and it helped keep her mind off— other things.

She flipped on the radio, letting the music fill up some of the empty space in the dreary room. Slipping out of her jacket, she shuffled through the stack of mail. Her fingers paused on an envelope with a Mansfield postmark. A mixture of dread and anticipation surged through her. Then she noticed the feminine scrawl.

She set the kettle on the stove for tea and curled up on the hopelessly modern vinyl sofa to open Leann's letter. A folded newspaper clipping fell out, landing in her lap. She ignored it, avidly reading Leann's newsy, homey comments about the town, her growing girls, Don's job. Leann knew better than to mention Jordan. The house was rented to a pair of newlyweds, she said, nice kids who showed great

180

signs of working out well and who didn't mind the weird black paint in the back bedroom. They missed her, and how was the glamorous life of a news photographer?

Kat's mouth twisted. She wanted to say "not so hot," but why worry Leann? It wouldn't do any good to say that the life had palled, the glitter was merely tarnished tinsel when compared to the things Leann had—a home, a family, a man who adored her.

Curiously, Leann didn't mention the clipping. Kat picked it out of her lap and unfolded it. Her breath caught and a heavy weight pressed on her chest.

Jordan's face stared up at her. He stood beside Dream Tender with the racetrack in the background. The filly had won a stakes race, generating much excitement about one of Mansfield's own.

Kat touched the blurred face with a trembling fingertip. Was he thinner? Did his cheekbones seem gaunt? Wasn't Bertie taking care of him?

She drew a shaky breath that was almost a sob and cursed herself for every kind of fool. Why did she still care? It only made things worse. She longed for his touch, to hear the deep timbre of his laugh. It wasn't his fault that he wasn't able to love her as she wanted. It was hell without him. Maybe she should go back. Anything with him would be better than this empty nothingness her life had become.

But, no. She was selfish. She wanted it all. And not having all of him would turn her into a bitter woman and eventually destroy the tender feelings. Without his total acceptance, there would always be suspicions in his mind, that niggling doubt that would sour and distort a relationship. She couldn't bear to see her love die an ugly death. What would be worse, Jordan would never understand when it happened. So she decided to take the hard road now and get it over with, never look back to what might have been.

Tears prickled behind Kat's eyes. She threw herself down on the sofa, her hair spilling over her face, the clipping crushed in her fist.

After a while, when the tears didn't come, she rose and went over to a cluttered bookcase. She pulled out a large manila envelope. Seating herself at the small, scarred desk, she removed the contents one photograph at a time.

Surely she had masochistic tendencies, she chided herself, keeping these pictures of a man lost to her. Jordan at the McElroy wedding, annoyed and stiff. Jordan laughing with baby Leslie. Jordan, proud horse breeder with a winning Dream Tender. She smoothed out the clipping and added it to the pile.

She should burn them. It would speed matters. But she couldn't bring herself to do it. Maybe in a few months, a few years. Or maybe not at all. Maybe these pictures would be the only things she had in years to come that meant anything to her.

Kat sighed, then carefully selected several of the pictures of Jordan with the horse. She hesitated a long moment over the note, and in the end hastily scribbled something mundane, then stuck everything in another manila envelope and addressed it to Jordan in her bold hand. She sealed it, attached the postage, then dashed, coatless, down to the corner mailbox before her courage could desert her.

Once back at the dingy apartment, puffing and chilled, she felt oddly content. It was a slender thread, those pictures connecting her with Jordan, and of no great significance. Yet, strangely, she was comforted, and she slept that night with peaceful dreams of Louisiana.

The pungent odor of sautéed onions and browning roux warmed the steamy air. Rosalind Scott paced restlessly while Bertie prepared gumbo in Jordan's kitchen. The only sound was the slap of the wooden spoon against the cast-iron pot.

"You don't like me very much, do you, Bertie?" Rosalind asked abruptly.

The spoon barely paused. "No, ma'am, not much. Never have, and that's a fact."

Rosalind laughed slightly at Bertie's blunt answer. "Well," she said on a shaky breath, "I don't much like myself anymore. I never meant to make Jordan so unhappy."

"Seems to me it's Jordan who should be hearing this," Bertie said. "He's in the office. Why don't you go tell him lunch is almost ready?"

"What could I say? That I made some terrible mistakes and I'm sorry?"

"That would do for a start."

"I wish there were some way I could make it up to him."

Bertie peered over her wire-rimmed glasses. "You can't blame all of Jordan's problems on yourself."

Rosalind looked up in surprise. "No?"

"I don't know exactly what went on between Kat and that boy, but it must have been pretty serious for her to take off the way she did. All I know is that those two young'uns are meant for each other. This coldness between Jordan and you has gone on long enough. It's time to see that he brings Kat home where she belongs."

Pale gray eyes met hazel ones and the two women silently agreed it was indeed time for action.

Rosalind found her son behind his desk, frowning over a large manila envelope. He looked up, dropped the envelope with exaggerated casualness, and stretched.

"Lunch ready? First cool nip in the air, you can count on Bertie making gumbo."

"Not just yet." Awkwardness colored their conversation, as it had over the past two months.

"So how's the campaign going?" he asked with forced heartiness. "Mel Stevens is lucky to have you working in his corner."

"Fine. He's very bright, outgoing. He'll make a good senator." Rosalind couldn't miss Jordan's suppressed agitation. "Is something wrong?"

Jordan looked startled, then the cool mask dropped into place. "No, of course not." His eyes flicked momentarily to the envelope.

"Is that from Katherine?" Rosalind asked quietly.

"There's no need to get upset."

"You haven't opened it."

Jordan's laugh was mirthless. He picked up the envelope, weighed it, tossed it down again. "I was trying to decide whether to open it or throw it away."

"Of course you must open it!"

Jordan's expression registered his surprise. "That's not what I expected from you."

Rosalind sighed. "Nowhere is it written that a foolish old woman has to stay that way. Life is too short, too precious to waste. I was wrong, Jordan, and I'm sorry. Maybe if your father and I had trusted you more with our problems, things might have worked out differently."

Jordan swallowed hard on a lump in his throat as he looked at the slender woman who had given him life. Conflicting emotions flickered across his face.

"I'm sorry too, Mom. I know it's been hard on you. I needed time to work things out in my head. I made my share of mistakes, including placing you and Dad on a pedestal, thinking you were perfect. I suppose that's one of the things that threw me so badly. It's taken me a while to accept that you're human, too." He came around the side of the desk and his smile was tentative, a bit crooked. "It's kind of a relief."

"Oh, Jordan!" Rosalind's eyes misted and she reached for her tall son.

Jordan felt a crushing weight lift from his shoulders as he hugged his mother. Waves of forgiveness and love washed away the estrangement, reconciling mother and son

184

and renewing the bonds between them. They pulled apart smiling.

"Well," Rosalind said, sniffing back a lingering tear, "aren't you going to see what Katherine has to say?"

Jordan's heart plummeted. He picked up the envelope and stared at it apprehensively. "I don't know what to do," he muttered.

"Maybe you'd rather be alone," Rosalind guessed. She bit her lip, hesitated, then plunged on. "I know you're miserable without her. And she left because of me. You've got to find her, tell her how sorry I am, and see if she'll come back. You have my blessing, for what it's worth, and I'll do everything in my power to make it up to you both."

"Thank you for telling me that, Mother. But it wasn't you, it was me," Jordan said, his voice low and tortured. "I couldn't give her what she needed."

"That's nonsense!" Rosalind scoffed, her mother hen's feathers ruffled. "You're successful, and handsome, and kind, and . . ."

Jordan chuckled, touched by Rosalind's ferocity. "Kat's perfectly aware of all my sterling qualities." His expression sobered. "No, it was my inability to give myself completely. I was always too cautious, holding something back in case of disaster, little knowing that *was* the disaster."

"Do you still love her?"

His eyes were bleak. "I've always loved her. She was the other part of me, but it's too late."

"No matter what's in that envelope, it's an overture. Do you think Katherine would make any kind of gesture if she didn't care at all?"

Jordan looked at his mother, then the envelope. A faint flicker of something hopeful and vulnerable flashed in his eyes.

"It's a chance, Jordan," Rosalind said softly, moving toward the door. "Don't let it slip away."

Jordan ripped open the flap of the envelope, then hesi-

185

tated. The muscle in his jaw twitched with tension. He forced himself to dump the contents out on the desk. Sandwiched between two sheets of cardboard he found the photographs, the ones Kat had taken that day at Louisiana Downs. He cast them aside, disappointed that they weren't photos of her. Then he found the note. It was painfully brief.

"Congratulations, Rusty," she wrote, and signed it simply, "Kat."

She must have heard of Dream Tender's win, he realized. Only that. A natural curiosity about one of Sabrina's foals, that's all it was. Jordan felt deflated, as empty as a child's broken balloon.

Something hot and wet splashed onto the back of his hand. He touched it curiously, then in amazement. A tear. Well, dammit! Why not? Couldn't a man weep when the sorrow went deep and pierced his heart? Wasn't there any release when he'd lost the only woman he'd ever loved? When he'd been a damn fool and thrown away the best part of himself?

Jordan thumbed away the painful wetness, grimacing when the moisture smeared the words on her note. He read it again, his lips twisting in bitter self-contempt. "Congratulations, Rusty." You've really done it this time, buddy.

Rusty. His eyes narrowed, his thoughts whirled. Rusty. Kat's pet name for him. The only person in the world who dared tease him, who dared—yes, for God's sake, say it!— dared to love him still?

Was he being a fool again? Dared he hope, or was it merely the ravings of a lunatic grasping at straws? She had every right in the world to hate him, to reject anything he had to offer. But he knew then that he *had* to make the offer one more time, and this time do it right. All of himself, everything, nothing held back in an all-out effort to make her see that at last he understood.

She had never needed his forgiveness. It had been his

own absolution he had been seeking all along. And whether or not she could still find it in her heart to care for him, the least he could do was tell her that.

"Hell, Scott," Mort groused, stubbing his cigarette out in an overflowing ashtray. "It's hard to say."

"Look, you people have been giving me the runaround since I got here!" Jordan snapped. He leaned over the desk and glared at the slight, balding bureau chief. "I've been to her apartment half a dozen times. I just want to know where she is!"

Mort shuffled through the papers littering the desk. "Well, let's see. What time is it? Oh, here we are. She and Scanlan should be at the airport. The prime minister ought to be making his final statement about now."

"Thanks." The single word was clipped, Jordan's frustration barely held in check. There was a throbbing in his temple brought on by his impatience to see Kat, his anxiety at what her reaction would be. But he hadn't considered that finding her would be so difficult.

"Mort!" A frantic young man burst through the door. "Just had a call. There's been an assassination attempt at the airport!"

"Jesus, Mary, and Joseph! Any casualties?" Mort was on his feet, his fingers punching at the phone buttons.

Jordan's heart lurched. Airport?

"Unconfirmed, but word is he's got a bunch of 'em pinned down. And our people are right in the middle of it!"

"Dammit! Keep your head down, Tony!" Kat hissed.

The younger man's face was alabaster white, and trickles of sweat ran down his face. They lay flat on their stomachs behind a loaded luggage dolly. Kat dove instinctively for cover at the first hail of bullets, dragging Tony down with her.

"What are they *doing?*" he almost whimpered. Kat

187

squeezed his shoulder. How many times had Bill played this role for her? Reassure your partner. Protect him. Your life could depend on it.

"Let security do the job. You just worry about staying alive."

An angry foreign voice spoke over the microphones where short minutes ago the prime minister had been outlining a compromise negotiated between two warring Mideast factions. Only a terrorist splinter group objected to this promise of peace—objected violently.

"What the hell is he saying?" Tony gasped.

"Something—something about making things known to the world . . . I don't know. My Arabic's kind of rusty."

Rusty. Oh, God, Rusty. The smell of fear and death was all around her. How could she bear to die without telling Jordan once more that she loved him? How inconsequential her reasons for leaving him seemed at this moment!

The ugly spit of gunfire rattled suddenly over her head. Kat lurched for Tony, holding him down with one hand, clutching her camera with the other.

Corridor sealed. No one in. No one out.

Jordan's gut wrenched in an agony of fear behind the security barrier. Where was she? Was she hurt? Oh, God, had he waited too late? Had it taken him too long to discover how necessary she was to his life? Had he missed his last chance? The litany beat in his brain: too late . . . too late . . . too late . . .

The sound of distant gunfire impaled him.

"It's all over."

The guttural voice of the SWAT team commander released Kat from her frozen, fearful state. Elsewhere other survivors moved tentatively, gingerly, with the quite real knowledge of their own mortality indelibly stamped in their psyches. Kat rolled to her feet, followed by Tony, shaken but intact. Her fingers moved automatically over the Nikon.

Out of the corner of her eye she saw an officer drop a cloth over a crimson-splashed body. The terrorist. The circle of bodyguards propelled the unhurt Premier toward the exit. She raised her camera, professionalism taking over.

Click. The ashen-faced but steadfast Premier.

Click. The coterie of guards.

Click. The silent body.

"Hey, you! You can't go in there!"

Click. The scuffle at the gate. Mort and—

Her shocked senses wouldn't believe the image she saw in the viewfinder. She pressed the shutter button, hardly knowing that she did, intent on capturing the hallucination.

Click. The tall man, running.

Click. The familiar, handsome face, strain etched harshly on each feature.

Click.

"Kat, are you all right?"

Jordan's hands gently pulled the camera from her nerveless fingers. His voice was ragged.

"You came," she breathed, awestruck. "I wanted you, and you came."

"Kat." His palms cupped her face. He looked at her assessingly. "You're really okay?"

She barely nodded, then his arms were around her, holding her so tightly she could hardly breathe. It was heaven.

"I was afraid I was too late. I've never been so scared in my life!" he said hoarsely. "There's so much to say, so much to ask." He pressed his forehead to hers and his voice shook. "I figured it out, Kat. Are you still waiting?" His words became hoarse. "Or is it too late to tell you I love you?"

Something beautiful and whole blossomed in her soul. "It's never been too late."

His lips found hers, a brief, searing kiss that burned away all the old hurts forever. She trembled beneath his hands and the silver promise of his lips. He threw his arm around her protectively, leading her away from the carnage and terror.

"I love you more than my life, Kat. Whatever you want is yours."

Her eyes were misty blue with love triumphant.

"I want to go home, Rusty."

EPILOGUE

"He's beautiful, isn't he?"

She smiled, her eyes following the new colt with the silvery, tinkling bell on his collar as he wobbled around the paddock. "He certainly is."

Her husband shook his head and laughed. "Not the colt —A.J.!" He pressed a kiss on the small head covered with coppery-colored fluff peeking out of the infant carrier strapped to her back. Bright blue eyes regarded him solemnly, then there was a gurgle and his tiny fist waved excitedly.

"Andrew John is beautiful, too."

Jordan's long arm gathered her to him. His warm caramel-colored eyes overflowed with humor and love. "Give up, kitten. He's stuck with A.J. And I don't think his namesakes would mind."

Her smile was tender. "No, I don't think so either."

"What are you two doing down here, anyway? Mother and Bertie are waiting, and you know how much effort Bertie put into that cake."

"I don't know, really. Just thinking, feeling, counting my blessings." There was a little catch in her voice. "Oh, Rusty, I never imagined I could be this happy."

"You aren't missing the studio too much?"

"I'll go back when A.J. is a little older. Leann has al-

191

ready offered to keep him. I just want to enjoy him—and you."

His eyes darkened with desire and love. He knew that this woman was all he'd ever need or want and he gave thanks each day for her. "That's the way I like to hear you talk, woman."

His mouth covered hers, sealing again the promises they'd made to each other that grew more complex, more compelling, more fulfilling day by day. A.J., too long ignored, kicked and crowed, swinging his tiny fists. They broke apart with the indulgent laughter of new parents.

"I have something I've been saving for you," he said. He dug down in his jeans pocket, caught her hand, then slipped the golden circle with the tiny diamond onto her finger to rest snugly against the wide gold wedding band. "It's rather a belated present, but I thought you should have it."

Her lips parted in surprise and wonder. She touched the ring with trembling fingers. "Is this the one that . . ."

"Yes."

Kat had thought that her heart was as full with love as it could get. Now she knew she'd been wrong. Her heart expanded with the knowledge that he'd kept this ring— this first love's, true love's ring—all this time, through good and bad, saving it for this special moment, for her. Whether he realized it or not, it was a gift of faith.

Her kiss was exquisitely sweet, filled with gratitude and joy. "I love you, Jordan."

He swallowed, his expression pleased. "We'd better hurry or we'll miss the party, kitten."

A.J. cooed his agreement.

"I've already had the best presents of all," she said softly. Jordan smiled and he kissed his wife tenderly.

"Happy birthday, Kat."